DEAD LAST

CROSSROADS QUEEN
BOOK 3

ANNABEL CHASE

D1737729

RED PALM PRESS LLC

Cover by Trif Designs

❀ Created with Vellum

CHAPTER 1

"Aren't you cold?"

"Of course she's cold. I see goose pimples on her arms."

"Pipe down, you two. You're killing the vibe." I kept my eyes closed and maintained the fantasy that it was still the height of summer instead of the end of October. The chill in the air promised that winter was coming whether I liked it or not.

"What if the swan sinks?" Nana Pratt sounded overly concerned given the size of the moat. This wasn't the Forbidden City.

I patted the sides of the inflatable black swan. "That won't happen. Gertrude is made of sturdy stuff. Anyway, I'm a strong swimmer."

"You named your raft?" Ray asked.

"No, I named my trusty steed." I would've liked to float out of earshot, but the ghostly duo could follow me wherever I went on this property, which was one of the downsides of buying a house next to a cemetery. In hindsight, I should've given the purchase more thought before I hit the buy button. Lesson learned.

"The children will be out and about soon. You should at least put a pumpkin at the front gate."

I flipped up my sunglasses to glare at Nana Pratt. "Why would I do that? A pumpkin is an invitation."

The elderly ghost appeared flustered. "Well, yes. It's Halloween. You're supposed to encourage them to visit."

"Lorelei didn't buy any candy," Ray said. "I peeked in her grocery bags yesterday as she was coming across the bridge. She had a loaf of bread, blackcurrant jam, unsweetened almond milk, chicken tenderloins, and a bag of mixed greens. No candy."

"Blackcurrant?" Nana Pratt echoed. "You must mean blackberry."

"It said blackcurrant."

"It's similar to blackberry," I told them. "I was introduced to it in England and like it better than the other kinds."

"And they sell it here in Fairhaven?" Nana Pratt mused. "Imagine that. I had no idea we were so cosmopolitan."

"There's an international shelf at the grocery store," I said.

"Didn't they have any international candy you could buy for the children?" Nana Pratt pressed. "They might enjoy a foreign delicacy in their baskets, like that Turkish delight Edmund so enjoyed in Narnia."

My gaze flicked to Ray. "Have you been teaching her how to turn the pages?"

Ray shrugged. "Gives me some quiet time."

"Gee, I wonder what that's like." I closed my eyes and tried to focus on the lukewarm rays of the sun. "I didn't buy any candy because I'm not entertaining trick-or-treaters. Besides, there's no way kids are going to trudge all the way up the hill to Bluebeard's Castle on the off chance I might be giving out treats. This place is too far from everywhere else."

Which was exactly the way I wanted it.

The Castle was a relic of the Gilded Age that I bought with money I'd earned in London. With a moat, an imposing iron gate, and five thousand square feet, it was more of a fortress than a house, which was the main reason it appealed to me. Unfortunately, the adjacent cemetery had saddled me with these two ghosts, Nana Pratt and Ray Bauer. To be fair, I could've forced them to cross over along with the other spirits, but when they respectfully asked to stay, I had a moment of temporary insanity and allowed it. Another lesson learned.

"Alicia will make the trek," Ray said. "She won't be put off by the exercise involved."

I hadn't considered that. I leaned back in frustration, causing my head to flop against the swan's long rubbery neck and bounce off. Knowing Ray's intrepid granddaughter, she'd lead a team of adventurous teenagers straight to my doorstep. A couple months ago, Alicia made the mistake of attempting to summon a demon at the crossroads in Wild Acres and had to be rescued by yours truly, along with the prince of hell himself, Kane Sullivan. It wasn't a practice I hoped to repeat. I didn't move to a sleepy Pennsylvania town to mix and mingle.

"She likes Snickers," Ray said. "I bet they're on sale now if you hurry."

"No, they're not," Nana Pratt countered. "They're never on sale until the day after Halloween. I would buy chocolate for half price and toss it in the freezer."

I lowered my sunglasses to the bridge of my nose to peer at them. "See? No point in going now. I'd have to pay full price, and you both know I'm skint."

"You had enough money to buy that ridiculous swan," Nana Pratt said.

I dipped my hand in the cold water and tried to paddle away from them but to no avail. That was the trouble with ghosts; a moat was no obstacle.

"I bought Gertrude on Amazon for mere pennies. I consider the purchase an act of self-care."

"I thought the moat was self-care," Ray said.

"No," Nana Pratt countered. "The moat is self-isolation."

"I didn't pay for the moat, remember?" I'd struck a deal with Fatima Fayez, a well-known figure in Fairhaven also known as Big Boss. Fatima agreed to have a friend upgrade the sorry state of my moat if I exorcised a ghost from a neighborhood house. The job turned out to be far more complicated than either of us expected, but in the end, I got my much-improved moat.

"Buy one bag of candy," Ray pleaded. "I can't bear to see the looks on their faces if they walk all the way here only to be given mints."

"Don't have any mints either."

"I used to give out Pink Lady apples," Nana Pratt said.

I turned away from her. "Of course you did."

"At least display a pumpkin," Ray said. "You've got a dozen of them growing in the field on the other side of the moat."

I sat up. "I have my own pumpkin patch?"

"In the backyard. You'd know that if you took any interest in the world outside your walls." Ray's tone managed to be both reproachful and sympathetic.

I contemplated the moat. "I don't know. I'd have to float all the way around back. That'll take time."

Ray heaved a sigh. "I can get one."

"Are you sure?" The ghosts had only recently started to develop their poltergeist skills. Turning the pages of a book was simple enough; moving a dense pumpkin to the front of the house would require greater skill.

"It'll be worth the effort," Ray said. "That way if any kids walk all the way here, they get to enjoy the sight of an expertly carved pumpkin. I've seen your knife collection," he added pointedly. "I have no doubt you can create a masterpiece."

No rest for the wicked. I paddled to the side of the moat and climbed out, dragging my swan with me. "If you're so dead set on it, why not make it yourself? You were a carpenter. I bet you could carve an excellent jack-o'-lantern."

"You can't expect him to have that level of control over a carving knife," Nana Pratt objected. "It isn't the same as pushing a book off the table."

"It isn't like he can hurt himself if he messes up," I said. "Might as well give it a try."

Ray seemed to warm to the idea. "And you'll put it out at the gate if it looks presentable?"

"Sure." There was no way Ray would be able to carve a presentable pumpkin. I predicted a smashed pumpkin and a string of not-quite curse words within the hour. Ray was partial to "dagnabbit" and "nuts and bolts."

I carried the inflatable black swan inside the house, otherwise one strong gust of wind would blow it away. It may have cost pennies, but that didn't mean I was willing to lose it.

I selected a carving knife for Ray and left it on the front porch for when he finally appeared with his prize pumpkin.

With the ghosts occupied, I returned to the kitchen to make a slice of toast slathered in blackcurrant jam. When I chose to move to Fairhaven, I didn't know about the powerful crossroads or the number of supernaturals that lived here as a result. Now that I did, I tended to keep my power dial turned to its lowest setting the way Pops had taught me as a kid. Despite dulling my shine, I'd already garnered too much attention. Vampires and werewolves sensed something about me that made them wary, although they didn't recognize what it was, and I had no desire to tell them.

My skin tingled; someone had activated the ward.

I shoved the toast into my mouth and chewed quickly before my unwelcome visitor made it to the front door. The bell rang as I swallowed the last piece. Victory!

I wiped the crumbs from my lips as I hurried to answer the door. Gunther Saxon stood on the porch. Wearing a full-length burgundy wool coat with a fur collar, the mage looked more like a runway model than a deadly assassin. His black hair was slightly mussed in a way that seemed like a deliberate style choice. The most interesting element of today's look, however, was the white bird tucked under his arm.

"You brought me a real swan for the moat? That's the nicest gift anyone's ever given me."

Gunther looked at the bird. "I thought this was a goose."

"No, it's definitely a swan." I paused. "Why would you bring me a goose?"

He shrugged. "Because they lay the golden eggs?"

Now that *was* a good reason.

He blew a weary sigh. "I know she's a swan. Can Dusty and I come in?"

"You named the swan Dusty?"

"Like you're one to talk," Nana Pratt interrupted. "You name all the inanimate possessions on your property. I heard you refer to the blender as Deckard, which seems an odd choice."

Not if you've seen Blade Runner.

"I didn't name her," Gunther said, oblivious to the ghost. "If it had been up to me, her name would've been Magnus. Maggie for short." He squeezed past me, prompting a dismayed honk from the swan. "Sadly, my parents had other plans."

My eyebrows inched up. "This swan is your sister?"

"Yes. Can't you see the resemblance? Same long, elegant neck." He set the bird on the floor and removed his coat with a flourish, revealing a grey and burgundy plaid suit underneath. He scanned the foyer. "You still don't have a coat rack?"

I took his outer layer and hung it on the corner of the open front door. "Ta-da."

"Where are your decorations outside? Kids will be swarming the yard in a few hours."

"If they do, they'll be disappointed."

Gun's eyes widened. "You don't have any candy?"

"Can we get back to the part where your sister is a swan? That seems more important."

He held up a hand. "We'll get to that. First, I'd like to know why you're denying local children their rite of passage."

"I have a collection of travel floss," I said. "Should I give those out?"

Gunther recoiled in horror. "I don't think I want to know you anymore."

"I'm surprised Halloween is such a big deal in Fairhaven. I would expect supernaturals to roll their eyes at the whole event."

"You have to remember, most people who live here don't know about the supernatural world or choose not to. For them, Halloween is a fun excuse to dress like us and gorge themselves on sweets."

"Nobody's dressing like you. They can't afford it."

Gun smiled. "So true." He pulled his phone from his suit pocket and tapped the screen.

"What are you doing?" I asked.

"Calling Cam for emergency supplies. She always has candy."

"I am perfectly capable of purchasing my own candy."

He glanced around us. "I beg to differ."

"Can we talk about the swan-shaped elephant in the room now?"

"I'll let her speak for herself." He produced a card from his pocket. Gunther was a member of La Fortuna, an ancient society of mages that used tarot cards to channel their magic. It was a practice I'd been unfamiliar with until I met Gun.

"Which is the Dr. Doolittle card? Is it the Magician?" I strained to see the face.

Gunther turned the card away so I couldn't see it. "There's

no such thing. The magic of the card is personal to its master."
He touched the swan's head with the edge and said, "Loqui."

"About time," the swan sputtered. "I could feel a massive scream building at the back of my throat. Seriously unpleasant."

"You haven't been able to talk until now?" I asked. I looked at Gun accusingly. "Why didn't you use magic sooner?"

"I did, but it doesn't last indefinitely. I figured I'd wait until we got here."

"And why are you here?" I wasn't magical. If somebody turned Dusty into a swan, I was hardly the one to reverse the spell.

Gun glanced at the bird. "Dusty looks uncomfortable on the floor. Can we talk in a room with furniture?"

"That narrows down the options to the kitchen or my bedroom."

"Kitchen it is," Dusty said, and waddled behind her brother to the adjacent room at the back of the house.

"Can I get you anything?" I asked as they settled at the table. I suppressed a laugh as Gunther pulled out a chair for the swan.

"No, thanks. We only want to ask for what we need and be on our way. I'd like to be home in time to give out candy." He cleared his throat. "Unlike some people."

My curiosity was officially piqued. "What is it that you need?"

The swan and her brother exchanged glances.

"Let me start at the beginning," Dusty said. "I got myself into a bit of a quandary."

"You don't say."

"I was caught stealing," she began.

"The criminal apple doesn't fall far from the criminal tree. Let me guess—you stole from a magic user who turned you into a swan."

"Not quite. I tried to steal from a wealthy asshat. His security was better than I anticipated."

"Clearly," I said.

Gun rose to his sister's defense. "Dusty is an excellent thief."

"What were you trying to steal?"

"That's irrelevant," she said.

"Not to me, or I wouldn't have asked."

The swan rolled her eyes, which looked more comical than it had any right to. "Fine. I was hired to steal artwork."

"Artwork? Like a Picasso?"

"Like a Judd Tyler."

"Who's Judd Tyler?"

"He's an up-and-coming artist. Very hot in the New York City art scene right now. Judd found out one of his paintings had been bought from a gallery by someone he considers beneath his work. He hired me to liberate it."

It took me a minute to collect my thoughts, of which there were many. "Let me get this straight. An artist sold one of his pieces, but he doesn't think the buyer is good enough to own it, so he paid you to steal it."

"That's it in a nutshell," Gun agreed.

"Couldn't he at least offer a refund if the guy returned it?" It seemed like the logical next step.

"Vincenzo Magnarella would never have agreed to that. He's as arrogant and stubborn as they come," Gun said.

So was Judd as far as I was concerned. "Does Judd Tyler know he can't control who owns his work any more than Nora Roberts can control who buys her books?"

"He was worried that the purchase would hurt his reputation and future earnings," Dusty replied. "Guilt by association."

"And sending someone to steal the piece back wouldn't?"

"I wasn't supposed to get caught." A regretful sigh whistled through her beak.

"I take it Magnarella has a magical security system that turned you into a swan."

"Wrong again," Gun said. "You really should stop trying to guess and let us finish the story."

"Then tell it faster." Patience wasn't one of my virtues.

"I was offered a deal," Dusty said. "Magnarella would let me off the hook if I agreed to participate in an experiment."

"She signed a contract without consulting me first," Gun added, with a disapproving glare at his sister.

"What kind of experiment?" I asked.

"I don't know all the details. Only that I made it to the patch test phase, which involved drinking an elixir," Dusty said.

"And that elixir turned you into a swan?"

She nodded. "Which means I failed the patch test."

"What was the elixir supposed to do?"

"Imbue me with the power of a god."

I balked. "That sounds like a dangerous elixir."

Dusty spread her wings. "Do I look dangerous to you?"

"I assume you were meant to have the power of Zeus."

She flapped her wings. "Sadly, this is all I got of him. No lightning bolts or anything cool. Not even a thunderclap."

"And you can't change back?"

"We've tried," Gunther answered. "The elixir doesn't work like a typical potion."

"And Magnarella can't reverse it?"

Dusty honked. "He can, but only if I'm able to find someone to take my place who can complete the experiment."

"Why not change you back and let you complete the experiment?"

"Because I failed the patch test. That means I can't continue, but he amended the contract to say that I'd turn back into a mage if and when someone else completed the experiment in my place."

"Like a feathered Cinderella at the stroke of midnight," Gun added.

"What a cunning prick. He's leveraging his own failure against you." I looked at Gun. "Why can't you complete the experiment for her?"

"Because I'm a member of the Assassins Guild. We have certain limitations when it comes to Magnarella. Honestly, if Kane knew about any of this mess, he'd go ballistic."

Kane Sullivan was the overseer of the Assassins Guild. The demon prince of hell was as feared as he was revered, and with good reason. I'd seen his flaming sword and his inner monster. Both were as terrifying as they were impressive.

"Dusty isn't a member of the guild," I said. "Why would Kane care that she tried to steal from Magnarella?"

"Because she's my sister. He'd consider it a violation of his gentleman's agreement with Magnarella to stay out of each other's way," Gun said. "My guess is Magnarella knew we'd want to keep Kane out of it and used the opportunity to make Dusty his lab rat ... or swan."

Wiley bastard. "Just out of curiosity, why ask me for help?"

"Because no one else likes me," Gun said.

"Bullshit. Everybody likes you."

He smirked. "I know. They really do. It's a heavy burden I must bear alone." He plucked a loose thread on his trousers. "It's because nobody else would've agreed to get involved and risk ending up on Kane's bad side."

I arched an eyebrow. "You think I want to end up on his bad side?"

"I think you aren't afraid of our demon prince, and he seems to like you. If he finds out you waded into forbidden waters, he may not kill you."

I grunted. "Death is the consequence for violating the gentleman's agreement?"

"Or banishment. Depends on his mood."

"He can't banish me from the Castle. I own it."

"Maybe so, but Sullivan owns this town in his own way. If he's pissed at you, you'll be packing your bags. Trust me. I've seen it happen."

I leaned my back against the counter. "What makes you think I'm not afraid of him?"

"Because I have eyes," Gun said. "I've seen you two interact. That isn't fear I see."

"Then what is it?" I asked, mildly curious.

"I don't think you want the answer."

"Gun says you two have the hots for each other," Dusty honked.

"Gun must be spending time in an alternate reality." My gaze skated to Dusty. "If you can't change back, how would you feel about living on my moat?"

The swan trumpeted.

I shrugged. "Worth a try."

"I'll pay you for your trouble, of course," Gun said. "Maybe then you'll finally invest in some furniture, or at the very least a coat rack."

"No promises. The list of necessities is long."

Dusty's gaze turned hopeful. "Then you'll do it?"

The combination of money and a swan in distress was too great to ignore. "I'll do it."

"Thank you, Lorelei," Gun said. "I know it's a lot to ask, payment or not."

It was, but I was also curious to discover what a dangerous guy like Magnarella intended to do with the god elixir. The best way to accomplish that was to participate in the experiment.

"We should get going," Dusty said. "We don't want to miss the trick-or-treaters."

Gun smiled as he lifted his sister off the chair. "Dusty's

going to sit outside and critique their costumes as they walk by. It'll totally freak them out."

I accompanied them to the front door, and we stepped onto the porch.

"Hell's bells!" Gunther lunged forward and karate-chopped a carving knife to the wooden floorboards.

"Hey!" Ray stared in dismay at the messy hole in the pumpkin.

"Ray was holding the knife," I explained. "He's making a jack-o'-lantern."

Gun groaned. "I forgot about your Caspers. I thought you had an invisible assassin."

"Methinks you're projecting," I said.

Ray picked up the knife and resumed his task.

Gun shaded his eyes against the autumn light. "Perfect timing. Here's Cam now."

The petite blue-haired mage hurried up the walkway carrying an orange and black gift bag.

"No shamans?" I said, as she approached the porch.

"Your house has been cleansed," she replied. "Anyway, I don't intend to go inside. I'm only dropping off your emergency candy." She thrust the gift bag into my hand. "You're welcome."

I looked inside to see dozens of boxes of Nerds candy. "This is your personal stash, isn't it?"

She shrugged. "It's what I give out every year. The kids go nuts."

"That's from all the sugar," Nana Pratt said.

I dropped the gift bag to my side. "Thanks. I owe you."

Camryn's gaze darted to Gun. "Did you ask her?"

He nodded. "She said she'll do it."

Cam broke into a bright smile. "I told him you would."

"You seem to know me better than I know myself," I said. "I never would've imagined saying yes to a request like this."

"That's because you're in Fairhaven now," Camryn said. "We look out for each other."

"They need to go," Ray interrupted. "I can't concentrate on the knife with all the chatter, and I'm running out of time."

I looked at the bag of candy in my hand. Now that I was equipped with treats, it seemed unfair to deny Ray a fair chance to complete the pumpkin.

"Let me know when and where you need me," I said, escorting my guests across the bridge.

Gun blew me a kiss from the front gate. "Thanks, doll. You're the best."

The swan whooped in agreement.

As much as I hated to admit it, it felt good to be appreciated.

CHAPTER 2

I tilted my head as I observed the incoming group from the safety of my front porch. "I think they're zombies."

"They're not zombies," Nana Pratt replied with a derisive snort. "One of them is wearing a petticoat."

"So, it's a Victorian zombie."

"I think they're just tired," Ray said. "That one boy is dragging his bag on the ground, and it doesn't even look full."

Nana Pratt clucked her tongue. "They work these children far too hard in school anymore. It's all about tests and rote learning."

I took a step backward. "We shouldn't have left the pumpkin by the gate. It's basically a Bat signal to every child in Fairhaven, encouraging them to come here." It had been a colossal mistake. I should've said no. When did I become so soft? Pops would be rolling in his grave.

Ray squinted. "I recognize that construction worker. It's Alicia."

Ray's granddaughter had a spring in her step, unlike her zombielike companions. She spotted me hiding behind a post and waved. She was either unaware of social cues or didn't care. My money was on the latter.

"Hey, Ghost Lady. Is Grampa here?"

"Naturally." I gestured to my right.

"Tell her I love the costume," Ray said.

"Your grandfather says he loves the costume."

"That's because he made it." Alicia held open her pillow-case. "Trick-or-treat."

"No way," the boy dressed as Zombie Spider-Man said. "You guys aren't for real."

"I told you he was here, Matthew," Alicia said.

"Then why can't we see him?"

"Because he's dead. Duh." Alicia shook her head like he was an idiot.

"It's Halloween," Matthew said. "Shouldn't we be able to see ghosts tonight?"

"That's right," their Victorian companion interrupted. "This is the night when the veil between worlds is at its thinnest."

I looked at her. "I hate to break it to you, but that's a belief, not a fact."

"How do we know you're not yanking our chains?" Matthew asked. "You could've set this whole thing up to fool us."

"Lorelei wouldn't do that," Alicia said. "This lady doesn't mess around."

Matthew jerked his thumb toward the jack-o'-lantern at the gate. "She carved a pumpkin and stuck a light inside so that it glows like a disco ball. Does that strike you as someone who doesn't mess around?"

"Alicia's grandfather carved that," I said. "I had nothing to do with it."

Matthew rolled his eyes. "Do you think I'm stupid? Let's go, Bonnie. If we hurry, we can still hit the houses on Walden

Lane. I heard the mansion is giving out full-sized Hershey bars."

It sounded like Otto Visconti had gotten into the Halloween spirit.

"Want to see the cemetery?" Alicia asked quickly. "I can show you Grampa's headstone. It's where I would hang out and talk to him before I met my ghost translator."

Bonnie and Matthew exchanged uneasy glances. "Maybe you should think about seeing a therapist," Bonnie said carefully. "I can ask if mine has any room for new clients. You'd like her. She plays computer games."

I thought Alicia might clock the girl in the face. I was pleasantly surprised when she thanked her instead. "I'm good, but I appreciate you looking out for me."

"This generation is so strange," Nana Pratt murmured. "In my day, it would've been horribly insulting. Only crazy people needed professional help."

"I think it's wonderful," Ray said. "Gives me hope for the future."

Alicia watched Matthew and Bonnie cross the bridge. "Those two are lame."

"They're not lame," I countered. "You tossed them a grenade and expected them to embrace it. It wasn't fair."

She adjusted her hat. "I guess I can see that."

"You don't need to stick around here," I told her. "I only have one bowl of candy."

"I'm not here for the candy." She took the box of Nerds from her pillowcase and dropped it into the bowl.

"Tell her to go with her friends," Ray urged.

I glared at him. "Did you not hear me just do that?"

"It wasn't very effective. Try again."

Alicia smiled. "Are you arguing with Grampa?"

"Why should Halloween be any different?" I observed her slow-moving friends as they passed through the gate. "Are they experiencing a sugar crash? They're like two sloths crawling across a field of glue."

"They said they didn't sleep well last night." She shrugged. "I slept fine."

"They were probably too excited to sleep," Nana Pratt said. "Halloween is right up there with Christmas for some children."

"I'm glad to see the hardhat fits," Ray observed. "Her head finally grew into it."

I relayed the comment to Alicia.

"This is probably the last year I'll trick-or-treat. Mom says I'll be too old next year."

"Nonsense," Ray scoffed. "You should trick-or-treat until you're sixty if you enjoy it. There's no age limit on fun."

I glanced at the older ghost. "Do you really believe that?"

"Now that I'm dead I do."

Nana Pratt nodded. "Death has a way of bringing life into focus."

"The cruel irony," I remarked.

Alicia pursed her lips. "I'm feeling left out of this conversation."

"I agree with your grandfather. Halloween is for the living. Go find your friends. If you don't think you'll do this again next year, you should make the most of it now."

Alicia swung the pillowcase over her shoulder. "Fine. It's not like it'll be hard to catch up to them."

"If you see any creatures that look too realistic to be in costume, walk away as fast as you can."

She perked up. "I thought you said Bonnie was wrong about the whole veil thing."

"She is, but some creatures are opportunistic. If they sense a lot of prey tonight, they'll take a chance."

Alicia scrunched her nose. "Prey? I don't like the sound of that."

"Good. Trust your instincts. If you see anything that sets

off your antennae, walk in the opposite direction and call me."

"Got it." Alicia cast a glance over her shoulder. "You should give out candy at the gate. It's a long walk to your front porch. Kids don't have time for all that hoofin' if they want to hit as many houses as possible."

Nana Pratt grunted her disapproval. "Why not just drive them from house to house so their feet don't get sore?"

"I think Alicia has a point," Ray said.

Nana Pratt folded her arms. "Of course you do. She's your granddaughter."

"How about this?" I said to Alicia. "I'll bring the candy bowl when I walk you to the gate, and if I see any kids on the way here, I'll linger."

Alicia beamed. "Deal."

"You're spoiling her," Nana Pratt complained.

I didn't respond. Alicia was far from spoiled. Outside of school, she spent most of her time home alone because her father lived in San Francisco and her mother worked overtime as a lawyer in New York City. The teenager craved companionship, not comfort.

Alicia managed to catch up to the slow-motion silhouettes. I was about to walk back to the house when a familiar SUV pulled alongside the property line. Chief Elena Garcia emerged from the vehicle.

"Happy Halloween, Chief. Everything okay?" I asked.

Her leisurely pace suggested everything was, in fact, okay. "Just making the rounds. I look forward to passing this off to the new recruit next year, but I figured I'd spare him this year."

"You finally hired someone? That's good news." The previous officer died under mysterious circumstances—well, mysterious to humans like Chief Garcia. The supernaturals in town knew Officer Lindley had been killed by a literal monster.

The chief nodded. "It took time, but we found the right officer for the job." She looked at my bowl. "Have you had any kids, or did you get peckish?"

"A handful. They were fine."

"I wouldn't expect too many. If they climb the hill to get here, they'll miss out on at least a dozen more houses, including a full-size Hershey bar house."

I cocked an eyebrow. "Someone sounds invested."

"I overheard one of the groups discussing it. They opted to stick to the main neighborhoods, as tempted as they were to have a reason to visit the Castle." She peered over my shoulder to the house. "A little skimpy on the decorations. You couldn't manage one of those inflatable ghosts or a smoke machine? Hewitt's had them both on sale last week."

"I've been avoiding Hewitt's. Every time I go in there, I think of ten more projects I need to do." The Castle was a money pit; there was no way around it. Still, I'd committed to building a home here, which meant I'd get to each one of the projects—eventually.

"I know the feeling. Every time I look at my desk, I see two more files that need attention. Officer Leo is going to save my sanity." She tilted her head skyward. "Nice night for the kids. I'm glad it didn't rain."

I followed her gaze to the full moon. I hadn't even realized. The wolves would be crawling the woods tonight.

The chief's phone vibrated on her hip, and she snatched it to her ear. "Chief Garcia." Her face tensed as she listened. "I'll be right there."

"Problem?"

"Fender bender. One of the drivers nodded off behind the wheel and hit a street sign."

"Glad it was a sign and not a trick-or-treater."

"You and me both." She contemplated the bowl. "Mind if I take one? I could use the sugar."

"My Nerds are your Nerds."

She snagged a box and shook it in appreciation. "Thanks."

"She's right, you know," Ray said, once the chief had returned to her vehicle.

"That she needs a sugar high to deal with a fender bender?"

"That you should've invested in one of those inflatable ghosts. They're not too expensive and they look festive."

I carried the bowl toward the house. "Why would I buy a fake ghost when I have two real ones of my own?"

"Someone is calling you nonstop," Nana Pratt said from the porch, where I'd left my phone.

I swiped the phone from the floor. Gun's name lit up the screen. "Hey."

"Bad news," Gun reported. "Magnarella wants to meet you in person before he'll agree to sign off on you as Dusty's replacement."

"Is that in the contract?"

"Provision 3(d)."

"This contract seems to heavily favor the party who drafted it."

"Magnarella is a mobster with deep pockets. I'm sure he has entire law firms at his disposal."

"When's the meeting?"

"Does it matter? We both know you don't have plans."

Ouch. "Just because it's true doesn't mean you need to say it out loud."

"Lunch tomorrow at his place. Noon. I'll pick you up at eleven-thirty."

"He's allowing me to bring an entourage?"

"Under the contract, Dusty is allowed to be present."

"What if he rejects me?"

"Then she has to find someone else until he agrees."

I groaned. "Theoretically he can reject everyone she offers. Is there a chance he's misunderstood and deep down he's a mobster with a heart of gold?"

"No. They're all land pirates."

I responded with an inelegant snort.

"But I don't think he'll reject you," Gun continued. "It's in his interest to find someone who can pass the test. He's not trying to stick it to Dusty." He paused. "Let me rephrase. He wants someone to drink this elixir and get a certain result. The more test subjects, the better the odds."

I agreed with him. Magnarella had wanted her to display the powers of Zeus. Dusty was useless to him as a swan though.

"Tomorrow doesn't give me much time for research."

"What's to research? You show up and dazzle him, then you pass the stupid test so my sister can stop being a bird."

I decided not to argue, although the idea of walking into a lion's den without learning about lions seemed like a bad call. *Know with whom you're having the pleasure*, Pops used to tell me. It was an adage that had served me well in the years since then.

I hung up the phone and debated my options between now and noon tomorrow. There weren't many.

I called Otto Visconti. Although the vampire was reclusive, he paid attention. He'd likely know something about Magnarella.

His housekeeper Heidi answered the phone.

"Is Otto available?"

"He's entertaining a guest at the moment. Can I take a message?"

"It's Lorelei. What kind of guest are we talking about? An overnight one?"

Heidi hesitated. "It's looking good," she whispered.

I thanked her and hung up. "Shit," I said.

"Language," Nana Pratt protested.

"I have a problem."

"Then use your words."

"I did. I said 'shit' to alert you."

"What's the problem?" Ray asked.

"I need intel about a local mobster, and I need it fast."

Ray's head bobbed. "Seems obvious to me. Talk to your devil friend."

"He isn't my friend."

"He played Scrabble with you," Ray said, "and he helped rescue my grandbaby. That doesn't sound like a friend to you?"

"Kane can't know about the situation. It would get Gun and Dusty in trouble."

"What about someone who works closely with him?" Nana Pratt suggested. "A good secretary knows everything her CEO knows."

She made a good point. Unfortunately, Kane's right hand was his head of security, and she seemed to hate me. Still, it was worth a conversation. A lifetime of lying meant I could conjure a believable story as to why I wanted the information. And Josie didn't care about me enough to probe any deeper.

"I'll leave the bowl outside. If anybody tries to dump the rest of the candy into their bag, you have my permission to go full poltergeist on them."

"Where are you going?" Ray asked.

"To a place I'm not wanted to ask someone who dislikes me a few questions she won't want to answer."

He chuckled. "Have fun."

CHAPTER 3

The Devil's Playground was busier than I anticipated given that it was Halloween. In my experience, supernaturals stayed home and avoided the whole scene. Instead, they spilled out of the nightclub, and the sound of rock music along with them. As I passed a trio of vampires, I noticed two of them were dressed as angels, and the third was dressed as a nurse with a blood bag. The nurse raised the blood bag in greeting. So much for a quiet conversation with the director of security. Josie would be busy tonight.

The bouncer's gaze skimmed me from head to toe. "You're not in costume."

"Sure I am. I'm dressed as someone who doesn't give a shit."

He didn't crack a smile. "Can I see your invitation?"

"Is that really necessary? We're old friends by now, Larry."

"We're not friends."

"But we could be if you opened your heart just a teeny tiny bit." I dug through my purse for anything that might cement our bond. I plucked one of the remaining boxes of

Nerds from the bottom and held it out to him. "Trick-or-treat."

He contemplated the offering. "I've seen Camryn eating these. I've always wanted to try them."

"Here's your chance."

Larry took the box and jerked his head for me to enter.

"I expect a full review by the time I leave," I called over my shoulder. That had to be the lamest bribe I'd ever successfully offered.

The volume of the music nearly blasted me backward as I entered the club. Clearly no one was expected to converse tonight, which would make my reason for being here a bit of a challenge. If I had realized the customers would be in costume, I would've donned my own disguise. Anything to avoid being spotted by the club's owner. Kane Sullivan would think I was here to see him, and I didn't want to give him that impression.

Orange and black cocktails seemed to be the drink du jour. They sported tiny bats on the end of the toothpicks. A nice touch.

I scanned the sea of masks and painted faces for Josephine Banks. I figured she'd be able to shed a little more light on Vincenzo Magnarella in advance of my lunch date tomorrow. Little did she know I was giving her an opportunity to prevent me from screwing up her boss's relationship with the infamous mobster.

I ducked behind a customer dressed as a unicorn to hide from the bar, where Kane was usually holding court. I wasn't sure whether he'd be dressed for the occasion or wearing one of his expensive custom suits.

I maneuvered my way through the closely pressed bodies, but I couldn't find Josie. It was unlikely the vampire would be dressed in a costume when she couldn't even wear a smile.

I tapped a passing waitress on the shoulder. "Is Josie around?"

The waitress shook her head. "She hates Halloween. Mr. Sullivan always gives her the night off."

Now that was the attitude I was accustomed to, although it sucked for me. I needed information and had precious little time to obtain it.

I surveyed the club, wondering if there was anyone present I could interrogate. In the end, I gave up. I didn't know too many residents as it was, and everyone here was in costume. Now I just had to slip out unnoticed by the prince of hell himself, which shouldn't be too tricky amidst all these crazy costumes. I was basically a shadow.

I threaded my way through a computer with legs, Marie Antoinette holding her head like a purse, and a variety of other interesting choices. The exit was within view. My heartbeat picked up speed as I closed in on the door. I nearly mowed down the Pilgrim that dared to step between me and my freedom.

"Pardon me, coming through," I announced.

The Pilgrim and his ridiculous black buckled hat didn't budge. Only then did I notice the familiar scent of musk, sandalwood, and pine. "Leaving so soon, Miss Clay? You haven't even had a drink."

Dammit. Thwarted by a Puritan. Wasn't the first time either. I had a high school experience that still brought a blush to my cheeks. Hormones were a funny thing.

I quickly found my voice. "I came to speak to Josie."

"She isn't here, I'm afraid, but how nice to know you two have become chummy. Why not join me for a drink at the bar? I was in the process of chatting with a friend when I spotted you."

"And you hunted me down?"

"I can't help my quick reflexes any more than you can help your inability to blend into a crowd."

I couldn't decide whether that was a compliment. "It's late. I should go."

He pinned me with those whisky-colored eyes that promised more passion than one body could contain. "Surely you can spare ten minutes. I promise not to make you bob for apples."

"Because it's a dumb game?"

"Because they're poisoned." He paused. "It's a crowd favorite, although I admit I never saw the appeal."

I debated my next move. I was already here and had fumbled my plan to avoid him. I might as well make the most of it. I could lie to him just as easily as I'd intended to lie to Josie.

I hoped.

"Interesting choice of costume," I said, as I let him escort me to the bar.

"You'd be surprised how many of these men made it to my circle."

"Oh, I doubt I would. I read *The Crucible*."

"Have you met my dear friend, the Cowardly Lion?" Kane motioned to the lionlike patron waiting at the counter. His didn't seem to be a costume, yet he wasn't a lion shifter either. "I'd like you to meet Lorelei Clay."

I waved at the lion. "Nice to meet you. Hope you find your courage before the night's over."

The lion pointed to the bar, where shot glasses had been placed in a neat line. "Working on it."

"He wants to ask the Scarecrow to dance," Kane explained. "I've offered to intervene, but he wants to be a big cat and handle it himself."

"If he doesn't hurry, the clock is going to strike midnight," I said.

"I won't turn into a pumpkin," the lion replied. "This spell is set to last until noon tomorrow, in case I get lucky."

If only Dusty could say the same.

Kane patted him on the back. "One more shot, and then it's time to make your move. I command it."

The lion's ears twitched. "I guess I have no choice then. Nobody disobeys a prince of hell."

Kane winked at me. "You would do well to remember that."

The lion opened his maw and dumped the liquor. "Wish me courage."

"You're halfway there," Kane said.

The lion staggered into the crowd, emboldened.

"I can't believe you're hosting a Halloween party."

He cringed. "Are you disappointed I didn't invite you? I assumed you'd decline. I know how much you enjoy your solitude."

"You're right. I would've declined."

"Then what brings you here to see Josephine?"

"I need a reason?"

"Historically speaking, yes."

I leaned against the bar. "Fine, I have a reason."

His mouth twitched. "And I suppose it's also confidential."

"As far as I'm concerned, my grocery list is confidential."

He chuckled. "Can I persuade you to try me?" He paused. "As a confidante, I mean. I'm very discreet when the situation requires it."

"I'm already here, so…" I shrugged.

"Right this way then."

He maneuvered through the gyrating bodies until we reached a doorway at the back of the club.

"I thought we'd go to the room off the lobby," I said, pointing behind us. "You said before that it's soundproof."

"It is, and it's also currently occupied. Unless you'd like to witness marital negotiations between a minotaur and a harpy, I'd suggest you follow me."

I trailed behind him along a corridor and down a spiral staircase to another door that required his palm print for entry. The door dissolved, and he stepped across the threshold.

"Where are we?"

"Welcome to home sweet home."

I stopped at the edge of the doorway. "You're inviting me into your private space?"

"You seem surprised. I've been in your home. Why not welcome you into mine?"

I felt uneasy about entering Kane's private accommodations, as though I'd be crossing a line I couldn't uncross.

He seemed to sense my trepidation because he crooked a finger. "There's no need for concern, Miss Clay. I won't be chaining you to the bed, unless, of course, you make the request."

"You'd be dead before you got the handcuffs on me."

"I didn't peg you as a necrophiliac." His tone was cheerful. "I feel like this is a real breakthrough for us."

I was starting to regret my decision to stay. I walked through the doorway and immediately took in my surroundings in case I needed to beat a hasty retreat. His home spanned the length and width of the entire club, giving new meaning to the term 'man cave.'

"This is the last time you get to mock the Castle," I said. "This place is basically a lair."

He held up a finger. "Ah, but I notice you omitted the word 'evil' from that statement."

"Just because you're a prince of hell doesn't automatically make you evil."

"How open-minded of you." He gestured to an antique liquor cabinet with walnut inlay. "Drink?"

"It won't make us fated mates or anything, right?"

He smiled. "You are the most paranoid woman I've ever met, and that's saying something. It won't make us anything except drinking buddies, which we've already been."

I admired an abstract painting on the wall. I wasn't a huge

fan of modern art, but something about the colors and textures spoke to me. "You have an eye for design."

He seemed surprised by the compliment. "Thank you."

"Maybe I should've hired you as a consultant for the Castle."

"You can't afford me or my exquisite taste, Miss Clay."

"I won't argue with that."

He poured Yamazaki into a glass. "Can I offer you something fruity or with bubbles? I'm all out of little umbrellas, I'm afraid."

"Good thing, too, or I might have to stab you in the eye with the toothpick end."

He resisted a smile. "Apologies. The women I generally entertain here seem to share similar tastes."

"I'm not a woman you entertain, Sullivan."

"No. I find it very hard, unless there's a Scrabble board between us. When should I swing by for a rematch?"

"My calendar is full at the moment. You'll have to check with my secretary."

Disappointment flashed in his eyes, and I realized he was serious.

"Sit, Miss Clay. Tell me what you need."

I sat as close to the arm of the sofa as possible in case Kane decided to plant himself on the cushion next to me. Thankfully, he chose the leather club chair. He looked at home in it, like he was born to sit in a sophisticated chair like that, whereas I looked like I was born to wrestle with IKEA instructions.

"I'd like to know everything you know about Vincenzo Magnarella."

Kane nearly spat out his drink. "Magnarella? What have you gotten yourself into?"

"He's invited me to lunch at his house." There. Nice and vague. No mention of Dusty or Gunther either.

"Why?"

"Why not?"

"First Otto Visconti and now Vincenzo Magnarella. Are you a Friend of the Vampires now?"

I didn't realize Magnarella was a vampire. This conversation had already proven worthwhile, although I'd have words with Gun and Dusty later for failing to disclose that fact.

"I can't help it if the undead are drawn to my sunny disposition," I said.

"As are the dead. It seems you attract quite a range of supernaturals."

"Like I said, I'm a ray of sunshine."

Kane studied me closely. "You're hiding something."

Always. "I'm going to choose not to be insulted."

"Are you dating Magnarella? Is this a blossoming relationship I should be aware of?"

I shrugged coyly. "Could be. How well do you know him?"

"Well enough not to invite him to any parties. In fact, I'd prefer our paths not cross at all."

"Because his suits are nicer than yours?"

He adjusted his cufflinks. "Impossible."

"What are your dealings with him?"

Kane sipped his whisky. "Nonexistent. We have a gentlemen's agreement to stay out of each other's businesses. That's the extent of it." He gazed at me intently. "If you have a problem with him, however…"

I held up a hand. "I haven't come here to be rescued. In case you've forgotten, I'm not a damsel in distress."

"No," he said quietly. "I haven't forgotten." Kane had seen me fight; he knew I could handle myself.

"It's just lunch." Not that it mattered. I could eat lunch with anyone I chose. Kane Sullivan had no power over me— and I bet that drove him nuts. A demon like him was accustomed to supernaturals bending the knee. The only reason I'd bend my knee would be to kick him in the balls.

"He's invited you to dine at his house," Kane practically growled. "What's wrong with the lovely Italian bistro in town? Nice and public, and the seafood linguini is out of this world."

"What do you think is going to happen at his house? I'm sitting in your house right now and nothing's happening."

Kane's face hardened. He didn't seem to appreciate the comparison. "Where Magnarella goes, trouble follows."

"Then I guess he and I will have that much in common."

Kane didn't smile. If he didn't like the truncated version of my story, he *really* wouldn't like the full one.

"I dislike the idea of your involvement with him," he pressed.

"You can dislike it from now until kingdom come. That's beside the point." I rose to my feet. "If you don't want to help me, I'll find someone else." I ignored the sound of the ticking clock in my head.

In one swift move, Kane shot from the chair and blocked my path to the door. "No need. I'll tell you what I know. Perhaps it will change your mind. Please, sit."

I returned to the sofa. "I'm listening."

Kane shifted in his seat, as though trying to force himself to appear at ease. "Vincenzo handles multiple counties in the area, including ours."

"Handles for whom?"

He waved a hand airily. "His organization."

"So he leaves the Assassins Guild alone, and in turn, you leave his unnamed organization alone."

"He occasionally hires one of our members when he needs outside assistance, so we don't function in completely separate orbits." His gaze intensified, causing a chill down my spine. "Make no mistake, though. He's nothing like me."

"In what way?"

"Despite our gentlemen's agreement, he's far from a gentleman."

"Then why not sign an official contract to stay out of each other's way?"

"It would be a sign of weakness."

I pinched the bridge of my nose and muttered, "Men."

He swirled the remainder of the amber liquid in his glass. "Why come here to ask Josie and not me?"

"Because Josie is brutally honest."

"And I'm not?"

"Josie's made it clear she dislikes me. She'd be delighted to tell me the man I'm about to break bread with is a monster and all the reasons why."

"And that's why you trust her?"

I nodded. "Absolutely. If Magnarella has a third nipple, Josie would lead with that. No cushion."

"I can work without a cushion."

I leaned back against the sofa. "Let's have it."

His grin was full of mischief. "Are you certain you're up for it? I'd be happy to provide a pillow."

"Dream on, Sullivan. I'm here for information. Nothing more."

Kane licked his full lips, and I realized how intently I was staring at the swipe of his tongue. He seemed to notice, too, because his lips stretched into a smug smile. "Hungry, Miss Clay? I'm quite confident I can offer you something that would satisfy you."

"I'm fine, thanks. I filled up on Nerds before I got here."

He pulled a face. "More than one? I wouldn't have thought they're your type." He stopped talking. "You've been sharing snacks with Camryn, I take it."

"She thought my Halloween stash was lacking."

"And was it?"

"I didn't want to encourage the children. It's a long walk to my front door, and they seemed tired."

"You haven't seen tired until you've been in my circle of

hell. You should see the way we…" He cleared his throat. "Never mind."

"Magnarella," I prodded.

"Right. The vampire is a caricature of himself. He likes cigars and brandy."

I blew a raspberry. "Typical. Next, you're going to tell me his favorite dessert is a cannoli."

"Close. Tiramisu."

"He can have it."

"Not a fan?"

"No. I think it's boring. Might as well eat cottage cheese and call it a night."

"Then what's your idea of a favorite dessert?"

"Anything with chocolate for starters. Bonus points if it has peanut butter or caramel."

"A real sweet tooth. Miss Clay, you do manage to surprise me."

"What about you?"

"I don't know if I should tell you. You'll accuse me of being bland."

"Vanilla pudding?"

"Close. Creme brûlée."

"I'll forgive you that one. It's better than tiramisu." My stomach growled, prompting a smile from Kane.

"Is all this talk of dessert giving you a craving?"

"The desire is always there. It's just whether I act on it."

His smile widened, and I replayed my words in my head. Damn demon.

Kane must've been feeling merciful because he let the comment slide. "Now, when are we going to talk about your other friend?"

"Which friend is that?"

"Because you have so many?"

"Hey," I objected. "Uncalled for."

He finished his whisky and set the empty glass on a

coaster beside the chair. "Your friend in Wild Acres who tried to eat the young girl. She recognized you."

"I don't think so."

"Then why did she bow to you?"

And here I thought I'd escaped that close call. A couple months ago Ray's granddaughter Alicia accidentally summoned a Lamashtu, bringer of fever, nightmares, and death. The creature recognized me and expressed her allegiance. I could have commanded her to leave the girl alone, but that would've revealed too much. I stayed quiet and was grateful when Kane intervened to dispatch the Lamashtu before she could hurt Alicia. Now it seemed I'd overestimated my stealthy sidestep of the issue.

"I don't know what to tell you. She obviously had me confused with someone else." I wanted to get up and start walking, but I forced myself to remain calm.

"Lorelei," he began. He never used my first name.

I kept my mask of innocence firmly in place. "Yes?"

"Whatever it is, you can tell me."

"I'd be happy to—if there were something to tell."

Kane shook his head. "Fine. I won't push. You'll tell me when you're ready."

Don't hold your breath, I thought. "That's an interesting attitude from a demon with an expertise in torture."

"The expertise belongs to my minions. I simply oversee, or I did when I lived there."

"And why don't you live there anymore? I forget what you told me." I slapped the arm of the sofa. "Oh, that's right. You haven't told me anything."

He allowed himself a small smile.

"Now, can we talk more about Magnarella?" I pressed. "My lunch is in about twelve hours, and I still don't feel like I know what I'm walking into." That much was true.

The demon seemed to accept I wasn't going to loosen my lips about the Lamashtu, because he switched gears.

"Magnarella is pompous. He has more staff for his house than security. He doesn't retain a bodyguard. I've been told he even brags about it, like it's a badge of honor."

"It's stupid."

"It is, but don't be fooled. The vampire himself isn't. He also has powerful backers and the kind of money that would make anyone superhuman." Kane hesitated. "It isn't about the money, is it? This desire to connect with him. If you're in need of financial assistance, I could…"

I shot to my feet. "Don't finish that sentence. You'll embarrass us both."

"Very well. Is there anything else you'd like to know that I haven't covered? I'm afraid I can't shed any light on the existence of a third nipple or any other part of his anatomy."

"I've heard enough, thank you."

He walked me to the door to rejoin the club. "Then you'll still go through with the date?"

"It's only lunch. I can handle one meal."

"Be warned, Miss Clay. Once you're in his sights, it's very hard to shake him. He's very much a predator in that regard."

"Good thing I have experience with predators then." I entered the club and immediately recognized the sound of Chopin's Raindrop prelude.

Kane noticed as well because he said, "Who let Bilson on the piano again? This is supposed to be a party atmosphere."

"He's rushing the composition," I said.

The demon shot me a curious look. "Is he? It seems to me he always manages to lower the mood to depressive levels." He made eye contact with the bartender who shrugged helplessly.

I was relieved to be going now. The song stirred up too many memories, and I wasn't in the mood to relive them.

Truthfully, it was best for everyone if I didn't.

CHAPTER 4

t took five minutes for my computer to boot up. I knew I should replace the ancient machine before its inevitable demise, but I was determined to stretch out its life as long as possible. My bank account couldn't handle the expense of a new computer on top of everything else. Every day there was some new expense I hadn't anticipated. A broken downspout. A cracked windowpane. Pops had made home ownership look easy, and maybe it had been for him. Not so much for me.

I logged into my bank account to confirm my suspicions. I blinked at the computer screen to see whether the numbers changed.

Nope. Still the same. Pitiful.

Finances weren't my strong suit. It seemed no matter how much I skimped and saved, it wasn't enough to preserve the money I'd made in London. I hated to admit it, but I was glad Gunther offered to pay for my help. I would've done it for free if he hadn't, of course. The money, however, was desperately needed.

I vacated the chair and opened the kitchen door. The backyard was eerily quiet, except for the distant rumble of cars on the highway.

"Anybody here?" I asked.

Nana Pratt materialized to my left. "I'm here, dear. What do you need?"

"Money."

"Oh, I'm afraid I can't help you with that."

"I'm spending more than I should."

Nana Pratt looked down her nose at me. "You might want to ask yourself if those blueberries really need to be organic."

Ray appeared to my right. "Have you considered a part-time job?"

"If this rapid depletion of funds keeps up, I won't have a choice." But then I'd fall behind on renovations. There was still so much to do.

"Why not ask your friend to pay you more for helping with the swan situation?" Nana Pratt asked.

"He's already offered to pay."

"I realize that, which is why I said to ask for more."

"That would be unethical. They're desperate. I'd be taking advantage of them." And I wasn't even certain how much he'd paid me. I didn't bother to ask since I was willing to help regardless.

"You're not a superhero," Ray pointed out. "You're allowed to accept payment for services rendered."

"Your time is valuable, Lorelei," Nana Pratt chimed in. "Don't undervalue yourself like the women of my generation. All the daily tasks we performed, day and night, and not for a single penny. And most times, all we got were dirty socks on the floor next to the hamper instead of gratitude."

"Honestly, it seems wrong to accept money at all," I said. "I feel uncomfortable about it."

"Does your friend Mr. Sullivan charge people to drink at his nightclub?" Nana Pratt asked. "Or does he simply throw a party every night and foot the bill?"

"That's different," I said.

"If you go to the doctor, do they heal you out of the goodness of their heart, or do they charge you for their time?" Ray asked.

"Okay, I get the point."

Nana Pratt peered past me into the kitchen. "You know, I was in charge of the budget for my family, and I was very strict. I'd be more than happy to take a look at yours and make some adjustments."

I looked at her through slitted eyes. "Would you make me sacrifice my organic blueberries?"

"Not if you insisted on keeping them, but then we'd have to tweak your spending in other areas to make up the difference."

"Come in, and we'll give it a try." I retreated into the kitchen and the elderly ghost followed.

I sat at the computer and pointed at the screen. "That's the money in my account."

"And where's your budget?"

I gave her a blank look. "I just showed you. That's how much money I have left. It needs to last as long as possible, taking into account the cost of food and house repairs."

Nana Pratt frowned. "How have you gotten this far in life without mastering the art of the budget?"

"My grandfather was focused on other priorities."

She tutted. "He did you no favors by ignoring finances. It was one good thing my parents did for me."

I didn't bother to defend Pops. She wouldn't understand how much of his life he'd sacrificed for me. To educate me. To keep me safe. Money had been the means to an end; it had only been important to him for survival.

"Less criticism and more constructive feedback, please," I said.

"I'll need time to work up a budget for you. I can't just snap my fingers like one of your magical friends."

"They don't snap their fingers. They use tarot cards."

"I'll also need to ask you personal questions." She observed me closely.

"Okay."

"Okay? Are you sure about that?"

I twisted in the chair to look at her. "Why are you saying it like that?"

"You're not exactly an open book. You get irritable when people ask you personal questions."

"If you need to ask me about present and future purchases in order to help me create a budget, I'm fine with that. Don't make a mountain out of a molehill."

She glanced at the counter. "Where's a pen?"

"Will you be able to write?"

"My poltergeist skills are developing nicely. They're not as advanced as Ray's, but I'm pleased."

"There's a pen in the drawer by the coffeemaker. Paper too."

It took her a minute to open the drawer and remove the pen and paper, but she managed.

"We'll start at a macro level, then go micro," she began.

"This sounds like it's going to take time. Let me put the kettle on." My skin prickled. "Actually, hold that thought. Someone's here."

I exited the kitchen and walked to the front door. A peep out the window revealed a middle-aged woman on the front porch. How did she get here so fast? Even at a brisk pace, she shouldn't have made it past the bridge yet.

The visitor was average height, with close-set eyes and brown hair worn in a severe bun. Her skin was unnaturally smooth for a woman who looked like she frowned a lot. She wore a black coat over a white blouse and wool trousers. Her sensible heels were too chunky to get stuck between the floorboards. She held a brown leather briefcase in lieu of a purse. Camryn would've cringed at the sight of the mismatched black and brown. According to the mage, a woman's bag should always match her shoes. I pointed out that designers didn't make handbags to match steel-toed boots. She told me with an air of haughtiness that I clearly hadn't been researching the right designers.

"I don't recognize this lady," Nana Pratt said. "Do you know her?"

Ignoring the ghost, I opened the door.

"Good morning," the woman said, with the faintest hint of a smile. "Are you Lorelei Clay?"

"Yes, and I feel obliged to mention the 'No Trespassing' sign you passed on your way through the gate." She moved so quickly, she might've missed it.

"I'm here to see you, Miss Clay. I don't consider that trespassing. And before you ask, I'm not from the IRS, nor am I trying to convert you to a religion or sell you anything."

I folded my arms and leaned against the doorjamb. "You've told me all the reasons you aren't here. How about the reason you are?"

"I'll get to that. May I come in?"

"Not today. I painted earlier, and the fumes are unpleasant."

"You haven't painted for weeks," Nana Pratt objected.

I kept my focus on the visitor. "We can talk right here."

"Fine with me. My name is Naomi Smith."

"How can I help you, Ms. Smith?"

"I'm conducting an investigation for my employer." She handed me a business card and my stomach lurched at the sight of the familiar symbol. "Two of our employees recently died, and I've been tasked with submitting the final report in order to close the file as per our protocol." She shrugged. "I'm sure you know how tedious bureaucracy can be."

I plastered on a mask of ignorance. "I'm not sure how I fit in."

She shuffled papers in her briefcase and produced a file.

"You were identified as an officer in training in the last communication we received from Solomon Shah. There's a copy in here if you'd like to read it."

I waved it away. "I don't know why anyone would say that. I have no connection to the police department."

"That's one of the reasons I'm here. I fact-checked the report and made that discovery for myself."

"I wish I could help, but I don't know what to tell you." I took a step backward and started to close the door.

Naomi placed her foot on the threshold in an effort to stop me. "I can tell you aren't human." The words tumbled out in a rush.

I paused, debating how to proceed. "And?"

"Neither am I," she said. "I guess we have that in common."

She was trying to ingratiate herself. *Good luck, lady. I'm in a fortress for a reason.* "Lots of residents in Fairhaven have supernatural blood. It's nothing special. I'm sorry I couldn't help."

She offered a pleasant smile. "You have my card if you change your mind."

"Have a nice day." I closed the door and backed away from it. "Is she leaving?" I whispered.

"Yes," Nana Pratt said. "Not even a backward glance."

My heart was hammering so hard, my chest felt like a construction site. "I don't think she bought it."

Nana Pratt floated closer to the window. "What makes you say that? She's already passed through the gate and gotten into her car."

I opened the door and stepped onto the front porch, where Ray was hovering. "Who was that?"

"Trouble," I replied.

Ray whistled. "Well, trouble drives a nice car. That's a quality Mercedes."

I wiped my sweaty palms on my jeans. "Mark my words. This isn't over."

"What isn't?" Ray asked. "I missed the conversation."

"She's looking into the deaths of Bruce and Solomon," I explained.

"Oh, the house on Thoreau Street?" he asked with mild curiosity.

I nodded. The complicated job that netted me the upgraded moat. "She's from The Corporation." According to Kane, The Corporation was a powerful organization that I definitely wanted to avoid. It probably wasn't the wisest decision to close their secret interdimensional bank vault in the basement of Bruce Huang's house and release the dragon shifter's spirit from the pearl in which it had been imprisoned by his employers.

But I'd do it again in a heartbeat.

"I don't see what you're worried about," Nana Pratt said. "She seemed friendly. What's the worst she can do? Insist you're a liar? I'm sure you've been called worse."

"Gee, thanks."

"She can't prove your involvement, or she wouldn't have come here," Ray added. "She needs you to confess."

Which I would never, ever do. There was too much at stake.

"If you're concerned, maybe you should call someone," Nana Pratt suggested.

"Like who?"

"Chief Garcia?"

I laughed. "I know supernaturals are still a new concept to you, but Chief Garcia is human, and she doesn't fully grasp the world around her." The police chief had no more than a vague awareness that life in Fairhaven was more complex than in other towns. To her, the existence of the crossroads was an historical footnote rather than a present problem.

"What about the devil man?" Nana Pratt asked.

"Kane Sullivan is a prince of hell."

"Isn't that the same thing?"

"He's technically a demon, not a devil. I don't think this is something he can help with." Although it did seem only right to tell him about the investigation. After all, he was the one who helped me clean up that particular mess.

I retrieved my phone from the counter.

"I wouldn't use the phone to communicate about her visit," Ray advised. "She might have left a listening device behind."

I spun around to face the ghost. "Boundaries, Ray."

"Sorry, you seemed concerned. I followed you to offer moral support."

"I'm fine. Go check on the scarecrow. It looks windy out there. Make sure Buddy didn't blow over." Now that autumn was here, it quickly became apparent that my herb garden was a big hit with the bird community. A scarecrow seemed like the obvious solution.

"You named the scarecrow too?" Nana Pratt asked.

"What's wrong with that? If we're going to dress him in clothes and a hat, then he deserves a name."

"I think you could've done better than Buddy," she said. "That's a nickname."

"Out," I ordered.

The ghosts fled the scene. I contemplated my phone and decided that Ray was right. Even though she hadn't entered the house, there was a chance Naomi Smith may have tapped my phone another way. In fact, I probably shouldn't have had that conversation with the ghosts on the front porch either. I'd need to hire someone to cast a sweeping spell to check for hidden devices.

More unanticipated expenses. Story of my life.

I'd alert Kane later. Right now, I had to shower and make myself presentable for the luncheon at Chez Mobster. I had no idea what it would take to gain his approval to replace Dusty, but I was guessing body odor wasn't on the list.

CHAPTER 5

As promised, Gunther arrived promptly at eleven-thirty to drive me to the home of Vincenzo Magnarella.

"I thought you'd be ready by now," he complained.

I glanced down at my blouse and jeans. "I am ready."

Disapproval marred his sculpted features. "You can't wear that."

"And hello to you, too." I widened the gap to let him pass.

"Remember, you can't just waltz in and take my sister's place. We need his approval, so you need to look worthy."

"I have no idea what that involves."

"Clearly." Gunther sighed dramatically. "I need to spend time in your closet."

I observed his fringe jacket and flared trousers. "It's too late for that."

He swatted my arm. "We need to tweak your outfit before we go. Dusty didn't catch his attention with her intellect."

"Hey!" the swan said. "I'm right here."

Gun looked at her. "Come on. You know I'm not saying anything that isn't true."

The swan tilted her head. "Fine. He likes attractive

women. If I'd been ugly, he would've punished me far differently for trying to steal from him."

I pressed a hand against my chest. "A powerful vampire mobster prefers the company of attractive women? Color me shocked."

Gun crooked a finger at me. "Makeover time, sweetie. Let's go, or we'll be late."

"And you don't want to keep him waiting," Dusty said. "He'll see it as a sign of disrespect."

In my bedroom, Gunther had a grand time rifling through my wardrobe. "You are in dire need of an update."

"Why? I wear the same clothes every week."

He glanced at me. "You do realize you're making my point for me."

"My house doesn't care what I wear, and this is where I spend most of my time."

He pulled a dress from the hanger and held it against himself. "This will do."

"For which one of us?"

He tossed the dress to me. "Put this on, then I'll fix your hair."

"Can I wear boots?"

He gave me a pointed look. "What do you think?"

"Doc Martens? They're almost shoes."

"Are you serious about helping my sister or not?"

I made an exasperated noise at the back of my throat. "You realize this is sexist, right?"

"I don't care. The only thing that matters is saving Dusty. If you had a sister, you'd understand."

"My best friend in elementary school hated her sister." I took the dress into the bathroom and closed the door to change.

"I hated Dusty when we were younger, but I grew to love her," he said through the door. "Now I can't imagine life without her."

I opened the door, fully dressed. "I'll try to make sure you don't have to."

"Would a bit of makeup kill you?" he asked. "Your eyelids look bald. Where are your eyelashes? How do you keep specks of dirt out of your eye without protection?"

"I could glue little knives to them, but then I wouldn't be able to see."

He grabbed my arm and tugged me into the bathroom, where he attacked my face with cotton pads and brushes.

The swan had made herself a nest on my pillow. "Great job, Gun. She looks like a million bucks. Magnarella won't refuse us now."

"Unless she misbehaves." He pinched my arm. "Don't misbehave."

I smacked his hand. "No pinching. I'm not your sister."

"Oh, he used to pinch me all the time when we were younger," Dusty said. "It was his own special form of torture. He'd even pinch me under the table when Mom and Dad weren't paying attention."

"I outgrew it," Gun said simply.

I noted the red mark on my arm. "Apparently not. Do it again and you'll be missing two fingers, which I think you need to properly hold your tarot cards."

Gun broke into a broad smile. "I have another hand."

Once the transformation to honeytrap was complete, we exited the bedroom and returned downstairs.

"You look beautiful, Lorelei," Ray said.

"You look like a hooker that hangs around outside those casinos in Atlantic City," Nana Pratt countered.

"That's very specific," I told her. I was surprised Nana Pratt had stepped foot outside Fairhaven, let alone made it all the way to South Jersey.

"Maybe a little more cleavage," Gun suggested. "If I had your boobs, they'd be on display more than diamonds at Tiffany's."

I pinned him with a deathly stare.

"Or maybe not," he mumbled.

Gunther complained about riding in my aging pickup truck. "If Magnarella sees this truck, he's going to reject you before you walk through the door."

"He's not pouring the elixir into the gas tank."

"I don't see why we couldn't take my car. At least it's fast enough to act as a getaway car if we need to escape."

I cut him a quick glance. "It's only lunch. No one will need to escape."

The swan stuck her head between our seats. "If shit hits the fan, don't worry about me. I can fly."

"Twenty miles per hour," Gun pointed out. "You won't get very far."

I followed the directions Gun had loaded onto the GPS. "Everything will be fine. No one will need to escape by wings or wheels. Remember, he wants this to work as much as you do."

The swan's head bobbed between us. "You're right. I'm just getting nervous, that's all. I'm starting to get a little too comfortable in my current form, and it's freaking me out."

Gunther kissed his sister's feathered head. "We've got this, sis."

The Magnarella compound made the Castle look like a hobbit hole. Enormous gates parted to admit the truck.

"Phew," I said. "I was worried the gates would reject any vehicle worth less than fifty thousand dollars." I parked outside the sweeping double staircase that led to the entrance.

Gun touched the dashboard. "You obviously didn't pay anywhere close to fifty grand for this piece of garbage."

"Hey." I glowered at him. "No more disparaging remarks about my ride or our deal is off. Gary does his best."

"Someone's touchy," he said, as he exited the truck with his sister tucked under his arm.

"I didn't realize there were any houses this big in Fairhaven."

"The house actually straddles the border of two towns," Dusty said.

We arrived at a set of oversized ornate doors, and I pulled the rope.

"Play nice," Gun reminded me.

"In other words, don't kill him?"

"That's a good start."

"No promises. If he serves olives with pits, all bets are off."

Gunther gave me an appraising look. "You have a lot of rules. It's probably best that you live alone."

"Rules are good." Rules kept me alive.

A slender, well-dressed woman answered the front door. "Welcome. You must be Miss Saxon's proposed replacement."

"Lorelei Clay, and this is her brother, Gunther."

"I'm Linda, one of Mr. Magnarella's assistants. Please come in."

She didn't look like much of a threat. Kane seemed to be right that Magnarella favored staff over security.

Linda ushered us into the grand foyer that resembled the lobby of a museum. It didn't surprise me that Magnarella was a fan of art. He certainly had the wall space for it.

"Give me one moment to inform Mr. Magnarella of your arrival." Linda hurried from the foyer, her sharp heels clicking across the marble floor.

"How many wings does this place have?" I asked.

"Five, so three more than me," Dusty replied.

"I'm glad you can joke about it."

"Humor is a coping device."

The sound of Linda's heels brought our conversation to an abrupt end. "Mr. Magnarella will see you now." She shifted her gaze to Gunther. "He asked that you wait here. He only prepared lunch for three."

"How much does he think I'm going to be able to eat with this beak?" Dusty objected.

Gunther gave her a silencing look. "Understood," he told Linda and nudged me forward. I scooped up the swan and carried her into the dining room.

They weren't exaggerating about the mobster's appearance. Vincenzo Magnarella had cheekbones that looked as though they'd been handcrafted by artisans with unhealthy perfectionist tendencies. Straight black hair skimmed a pair of broad shoulders. His suit looked expensive enough to rival a year of college tuition.

His dark eyes twinkled with amusement at the sight of the swan. "I'll be honest. I did not have swan on my bingo card."

Dusty opened her beak to protest, and I quickly closed it. "Mr. Magnarella, my name is Lorelei Clay. I'm here on behalf of Dusty Saxon. I'd like to officially request your approval to take her place." I hovered awkwardly beside the table, uncertain whether to give the swan her own chair or hold her on my lap.

The vampire saved me from the indignity by signaling to one of his staff. "A booster seat for Miss Saxon, please." He gestured to the chair adjacent to his. "Sit, Miss Clay. Let us get to know each other over a good meal before we make any decisions."

The good meal was no joke. The penne was served with lobster and a vodka sauce and there were more side dishes than I could attempt to try. I enjoyed dining at Otto Visconti's house because of the delicious offerings, but Vincenzo Magnarella put the other vampire to shame, not that I would ever admit it to Otto. The cursed vampire was too sensitive.

"Red or white wine?" the vampire asked. "I'm not a purist when it comes to pairings."

"As long as there's brandy afterward, I don't mind."

His smile widened. "A woman after my own heart."

"For now, a glass of the pinot grigio, please." And I'd

watch to make sure nobody spiked it before the wine glass made its way to me. The last thing I needed was to wake up in a basement prison, or worse.

A figure darted forward and uncorked the bottle before I could reach for it. I'd rather struggle with a corkscrew for eternity than surround myself with others.

Magnarella noticed. "You seem uncomfortable, Miss Clay. Is it nerves?"

"Not at all."

"Well, I can see something is bothering you. I'd like this luncheon to be a pleasant experience for you."

"Fine." I waved a hand airily. "It's all these extra bodies in the room. Your lifestyle would suffocate me."

Laughter exploded from his full lips. "I see. Not a social creature then."

"Not by choice."

"Just out of curiosity, how did you make the acquaintance of Miss Saxon?"

"I met her brother when he was attacking a man on my property. We became friends."

Magnarella laughed again. "I didn't think you were one of them."

"One of them?" I queried.

"An assassin."

"No. I understand that would be against the rules."

"Indeed. And what makes you think you're capable of serving in Miss Saxon's place?"

"I was the only one willing." I realized the answer was vague, but I didn't want to say one word more than necessary.

He scrutinized me. "Do you have magic?"

"No."

"Then I don't see how you can replace her."

"I have supernatural blood, and I drink an elixir. What else is there?"

"You need to be strong enough to drink it in the first place. We don't allow humans for that reason." He inclined his head toward the swan. "Not all complications are as amusing as Miss Saxon's."

"Doesn't seem very funny to me," she grumbled.

I speared a piece of penne. "I'm willing to take the risk."

"You'd need to sign the amendment to her contract."

"I figured."

He pondered me, and I could tell he was trying to identify my species. I kept the dial turned down as low as possible. There were reasons Pops insisted I learn to control my powers, and vampires like Magnarella was one of them.

"Where are you from, Miss Clay?" He'd decided to take the indirect route, it seemed.

"All over. Most recently I lived in London."

"What did you do there?"

"I tracked down lost heirs."

He made a noise of interest. "And were you good at your job?"

"Very."

"That's a transferable skill. Have you opened a business here?"

"No, I wanted a change."

"Then you've come to the right place. Changing lives is what I do best."

Since he seemed chatty, I decided to ask questions. "What happens if I drink the elixir and get the qualities you were hoping for?"

"Patience, Miss Clay. We're still enjoying our food." He raised his glass of wine in salute and drank.

Dusty stuck her beak in a goblet of white wine and slurped. Any sense of shame had flown out the window at the sight of an expensive vintage. She was her brother's sister.

"I hope dessert is tiramisu," I said. "It's my favorite."

Magnarella's dark eyes lit up. "We should dine together again soon."

"That depends."

"On what?"

"On whether you let me take Dusty's place."

His gaze skimmed my face, down my neck to my cleavage. "You'll enjoy another meal with me if I agree?"

I lifted my glass and offered a demure smile. "Anytime, my liege."

"Business first." He snapped his fingers, and a staff member delivered his phone on a silver platter. "I have a firm policy regarding no devices at the table," he explained as he tapped the screen. "Benito, I'll need to amend Miss Saxon's contract to include Miss Clay as her proxy. Can you make that change and send it directly to the dining room? Thank you." He set the phone back on the platter, and it was promptly whisked away.

"You'll change Dusty back to a mage now?" It couldn't hurt to ask.

"Not yet. First, we must make sure you're a viable candidate. That requires an assessment. Then you need to drink the elixir without complications and complete the experiment."

A man hurried into the room with a document and set the contract beside my plate.

"You're welcome to have your attorney review it before you sign, of course," Magnarella said.

I accepted the proffered pen. "I know how to read a contract."

"I like a woman with intellectual confidence. Very appealing." He dabbed at the sides of his mouth with a linen napkin. "I think you'll do quite well in Miss Saxon's stead."

"Let's hope," I said.

"You'll meet with Albert in the morning for a physical exam. If you have any underlying health conditions, now would be the time to admit them."

"I'm in good shape."

His gaze raked over me again. "Yes, that much is clear."

"And if I pass the physical?"

"Then we'll discuss next steps." He tossed the napkin on his empty plate. "Be here at seven tomorrow morning. Wear comfortable clothing. Something that allows you to undress quickly."

I winked at him. "I always do."

"You can stop flirting now," Dusty whispered. "You sealed the deal."

Not yet I didn't. One step down. Two to go—if we were lucky.

CHAPTER 6

Nana Pratt stared at the bouquet of daisies in front of her headstone. "I'd prefer gladiolus next time."

"It's not the best time of year for gladiolus, but I'll see what I can do." The elderly ghost had requested that I "spruce up" her headstone in the cemetery so that it didn't look neglected. I agreed in exchange for her silence before ten each morning. I tended to be grumpy in the early hours, and her incessant chatter didn't improve my mood.

"You should relocate the scarecrow," she said. "The birds have migrated to the other field around back."

"I'm not protecting crops. Why not let them be?"

She bristled with anger. "I haven't been spending all my time helping you fix up this yard just to watch it fall prey to a flock of greedy birds."

"You're a ghost, Nana Pratt. All you have is time to spend."

She looked away from me, momentarily distracted. "Oh, my! The handsome werewolf is coming up the walkway." She still seemed to get a thrill out of the presence of shapeshifters in town. I had a feeling Nana Pratt had carnal desires she'd left unexplored during her lifetime.

Sure enough, I peered around the corner of the house to see Weston Davies, alpha of the Arrowhead Pack, striding toward the front porch. He wore the tight jeans he favored, along with a T-shirt that spanned his six-pack beneath a black jacket. His light brown hair curled at the edges, like he'd recently stepped out of the shower. His rugged jawline was covered in five o'clock shadow.

I let loose a shrill whistle and waved.

"That wasn't very ladylike," Nana Pratt admonished me as West turned and headed in my direction.

"When have you seen me do anything ladylike?"

The elderly ghost appeared thoughtful. "You wore a dress to lunch today."

"That wasn't my choice."

"Did you whistle at me because I'm a werewolf?" West demanded.

Oops. "Not at all. It was the most effective way to get your attention."

West glanced at the daisies on the ground. "Pretty. Daisies are underrated."

I shot Nana Pratt a triumphant look. The ghost dissipated in protest.

"I hope you don't mind that I dropped by unannounced," he continued.

"Everyone else ignores the 'No Trespassing' sign. Why shouldn't you?"

"I didn't think it applied to visitors. It isn't like I'm trying to sell you something."

"No, but I'm guessing you'd like my help with a problem, which is almost the same thing."

He seemed to take that on board. "Actually, I came here to share information."

"Is this about the Welshes selling their house because the husband was caught cheating with his secretary? If so, I got all caught up at the grocery store."

He stared at me for a beat. "That's not information. That's gossip."

"Isn't it the same thing?"

"Not to me." He paused. "Something strange is happening."

I feigned shock. "In Fairhaven? Never."

"No need for sarcasm. I thought you'd want to know."

"Why?"

West seemed taken aback by the question. "Because you live here now."

"I live alone in the Castle."

"The Ruins."

"Castle," I stressed, "with high walls, a gate, and a functional moat. Which part of that suggests I'm interested in outside events?"

He cast a quick glance at the moat. "It looks great, by the way. Whoever you used did a good job."

"Thanks. I'm happy with it."

West tugged his earlobe. "Are we done with the pleasantries now? I have information to share."

I sighed. "If you must."

"A few wolves slept through the night last night."

"Congratulations. They're big kids now."

He pointed to the clear blue sky. "It was a full moon."

It was. I'd seen it myself.

"Too much partying at Arrowhead Trailer Park? Too many beers can put me in a coma. I snore, too, apparently."

His expression remained impassive.

"Are they awake now?" I asked.

He nodded. "But they said they're tired. Said they didn't sleep well, which makes no sense. They slept like the dead."

An uneasy feeling gnawed at my stomach. "Have they been dragging themselves around today like sloths with brick feet?"

"More or less. One of them fell asleep in the kitchen,

which wouldn't have been the worst thing except he was in charge of making the oatmeal for everybody." West shook his head ruefully. "I haven't seen that much oatmeal on a body since before the chicken pox vaccine."

"How old are you?"

"Older than I look."

I digested his information. There was no way it was a coincidence. He was right; something strange was happening in Fairhaven. Again.

"Mind if I speak to the sleepyheads?"

West angled his head. "You know something?"

"Not exactly, but I don't think this is an isolated incident."

"That's what my guts says too. Come on, I'll drive you."

We exited the cemetery and crossed the bridge. "You're right about this place," he said, as we passed through the iron gate. "It's starting to look more presentable."

"Then you'll stop calling it the Ruins?"

He smirked. "Old habits die hard." He opened the passenger door of his truck for me; it was much newer and nicer than mine.

"Thank you, kind sir." The interior reeked of onions and garlic. "Are you defending your vehicle against vampires?"

He chuckled. "No, it's my turn to cook dinner. I stopped at the store before I came here to see you."

"An alpha that cooks," I remarked.

West turned the car onto the road. "I do it all. No one is superior to anybody else in the pack."

"Except they call you alpha. Is everybody else called alpha too?"

"The pack needs leadership, but it doesn't have to be as much of a hierarchy as people think to be strong and fully functional."

"Who taught you that?"

His face hardened. "A poorly run pack."

I'd forgotten until now that West hadn't grown up here.

He'd been a member of a different pack somewhere else when he was younger. I couldn't recall the details.

"Who's the pack treasurer?"

He shot me a curious look. "Dare I ask why?"

"I'm learning how to budget. I thought maybe they could give me some tips."

"He can certainly do that." He straightened his shoulders. "It's me. I'm the treasurer."

"You're the alpha. How can you also be the treasurer? Isn't that a conflict of interest?"

"We're not a company. I'm the one with a finance degree."

"You went to college?"

"I can't decide whether to laugh or be insulted. Yes, I went to college. Do you think all werewolves are ignorant imbeciles?"

"Of course not. I didn't go to college."

He glanced at me as he turned the wheel. "Why not? You seem smart."

"It wasn't in the cards for me." The moment I turned eighteen, I kissed foster homes goodbye and never looked back. College would've been another uncomfortable experience of sharing space with strangers. I didn't want it. I only wanted to be on my own, like Pops had taught me.

"I encourage all our wolves to attend college if higher education interests them. Trade school's good, too. We pool our resources so that everyone who wants to go, can afford to go. We do the same for trade schools."

"And here I thought you were a democratic pack when you're clearly communists."

He laughed. "We support each other. Nothing wrong with that."

"I completely agree."

He arched an eyebrow. "Really?"

"Why wouldn't I?"

"You seem very firmly in the Ayn Rand camp."

"That sounds like the least fun camp ever."

"You know what I mean. There's no 'I' in 'we.' That sort of thing."

"All this because I live alone? Sheesh."

He wisely decided to switch back to the topic of the budget. "If you're worried about money, maybe you should think about a part-time job."

"I'm not worried," I lied. "I'm trying to plan better. My old system isn't working for me anymore." In more ways than I cared to count.

He turned onto a dirt road.

"Your old system involved a job, didn't it? Tracking lost heirs in London?"

"Yes." I didn't want to explain my reasons for avoiding the job market. They would only result in more questions. West wasn't one to cut me any slack either. He'd made that clear. He sensed something was off with me, and he didn't want my presence to stir up trouble. If it were up to him, I'd get a job far away and leave town. As much as I respected his devotion to his pack, I wasn't going anywhere. Like he said earlier, Fairhaven was my home now.

The horseshoe-shaped trailer park was located on the wooded outskirts in the northwest corner of Fairhaven, south of the highway. There were about three dozen trailers total. He parked in the short driveway of his trailer, which looked identical to the others except for the looped iron symbol affixed to the front door that indicated his alpha status. Subtle, just like West.

I started toward the front door.

"Not there. We're going to the meeting hall." He pointed to a trailer at the end of the row where a small group had gathered outside. I recognized two of them: beefy Bert and Anna Dupree, a middle-aged brunette I'd first met at Monk's, where I'd demonstrated just enough power to bring her to heel.

"This seems very official. I thought we were having an informal chat with the sleepy werewolves."

"That's not how we handle our internal affairs." West cut through the visitors to open the door. "Sorry I'm a few minutes late."

"Why'd you bring her?" a teenaged male asked. I didn't miss the judgmental tone in his voice.

"Because she's a problem solver," West said.

"Last I checked, the pack solves its own problems," he shot back.

"Haven't I taught you better than that? It isn't weak to ask for help when you need it, Xander," West replied. "It's a sign of strength."

I looked at him askance. "Kane wasn't kidding about you."

"In what way?"

"When he called you a democratic leader."

West examined me. "You and Kane were talking about me?"

"Do you care?"

He shrugged. "Not really. I was only curious."

Everyone filed into the trailer. The only contents inside were a large, oblong table and twelve chairs. Not even a valance over the window, not that I should judge. My house was still more of a shell than a home, but at least I was working on improvements. I had a feeling this trailer was designed to be barebones on purpose. No distractions from the matter at hand. I bet West scowled at anybody who deviated from the designated topic until they stopped talking.

West indicated the chair next to his, and I took a seat.

"Can we get started?" an older woman asked. "I have a basket of vegetables that aren't going to chop themselves and these arthritic hands aren't as agile as they used to be."

"It's my day to cook," West replied.

"And I'm on the roster for sous chef duties," she said. "Didn't you look?"

"We'll keep this brief, Dottie. Promise." West cleared his throat and addressed the other attendees. "As you can see, Lorelei Clay has joined us today to discuss the sleep issue."

"If you're going to bring in an outsider, why not ask a healer?" Anna piped up. No doubt she didn't want me involved because she was afraid of me. Smart wolf.

West was oblivious to the real reason for her objection. "Because I don't think a healer is what we need," he said.

"I'd like to ask a few questions, if you don't mind," I interjected.

West quickly added, "You'll all get your chance to ask questions at the end of the meeting." He knew his audience.

"You're the one who said you didn't even want her here, and now you're inviting her to meetings," Xander grumbled. "I don't get it."

West's face turned stony. "Outside. Now."

The young werewolf looked ready to melt into his chair. "What?"

"We're here to solve problems, not create new ones. You're no longer welcome at this meeting. Now get out before I throw you out myself."

Okay, maybe not entirely democratic.

The outspoken werewolf slunk out the door without a backward glance.

"Xander's young and headstrong," Dottie whispered. "Don't be so hard on him."

"The fact that he's young and headstrong is exactly why I need to be hard on him." West rose to his feet. "Anybody else want to question me or complain about the way I'm addressing the current issue?"

The wolves suddenly found the wood grain on the table fascinating.

"Lorelei, you have the floor," West said in a quiet voice.

I turned my attention to the rest of the werewolves. "I understand there's a sleep problem affecting the pack."

"Not the whole pack," Anna said. "West only invited those of us affected."

I counted five if I included the hot-tempered outcast. "And you all missed the full moon last night?"

Heads bobbed.

"Normally, I'd run all night when there's a full moon," Bert said. "It's the night I have the most energy."

"Do any of you remember your dreams?" I asked.

"I didn't dream," a young woman said. "I slept like a rock. My mind was nothing but a big black hole."

"Same as Shoshanna," Anna chimed in. "But I don't get why I'm so tired. I slept ten hours. I should be refreshed."

No dreams. Still tired.

"And you're the only ones who've experienced this?" I asked.

"As far as we know," West replied. "I held a meeting, and they were the ones who raised their hands."

"Do you have anything in common from the night before?" I prodded. "Did you eat the same food or watch the same show?"

"Most of us ate the same meal and watched the same show," Shoshanna said. "It was family night."

Family night. How sweet.

"Nobody went trick-or-treating?" I asked.

"We don't participate in that," West said. "It's for humans."

"A lot of events are for humans, but you show up anyway," I pointed out.

"No trick-or-treating," West confirmed. "The pups painted pumpkins and baked cupcakes right here."

"There was an accident last night," I said.

"What about it?"

"The driver fell asleep behind the wheel."

"We live in a capitalist society," West said. "Everybody is overtired from trying to make ends meet."

"I was in town yesterday and half the people I passed seemed to be yawning," Dottie said. "That's not normal."

Now that I thought about it, I'd noticed the same thing. "No, it isn't."

West looked at me. "What are we dealing with?"

I shrugged. "Could be a million options. A Sleeping Beauty spell maybe."

"What's that?" West asked.

"The one where the fairies put the kingdom to sleep," I explained.

"Why would anybody do that?"

"I don't know. You want ideas. I'm just spitballing." I wasn't even sure that was a real spell.

"They're not staying asleep," West said. "They're asleep longer than normal, don't remember their dreams, and then wake up sluggish."

An idea occurred to me. "They either don't remember their dreams, or they don't have any?"

West noticed my thoughtful expression. "What are you thinking?"

"Let me get back to you." I turned back to the group. "I'd like you to keep a sleep log for the next few days. Note how many hours you sleep, whether you dream, and whether you feel rested when you wake up."

"Would you like the details of our dreams?" Bert asked with a wolfish grin. I could tell where this was going.

"That won't be necessary," I said. "Just the basic information."

"Shoshanna, you'll be in charge of collecting the data," West ordered.

Bert's hand shot in the air. "I volunteer as messenger."

"I'll give the data to Lorelei," West said.

The werewolf muttered under his breath as he lowered his hand.

"Unless there's anything else, this meeting is adjourned," West continued.

The pack members couldn't seem to leave the meeting fast enough, except for the one who seemed determined to get my attention. Naturally, I ignored him.

"Need a ride home?" West asked.

"I'm not going home yet."

West's brow furrowed. "Can you tell me anything based on what you heard?"

I chose my words carefully. "Not yet, but whatever it is, it isn't good."

West offered a wry smile. "In this town, it never is."

I decided to stop by the coffee shop before I hit the books in the library. I was surprised to see Naomi Smith inside Five Beans, chatting with Chief Garcia. The investigator smiled when she noticed me.

"Miss Clay, how nice to see you again."

"You're still in town," I said.

"I am. I'm staying in the cutest B & B," she said. "I'll be sad to leave it. The breakfast is divine."

Did my ears deceive me or did she stress the word 'divine?'

Chief Garcia took a sip of her coffee. "You two know each other?"

"We met briefly," Naomi said.

The chief's eyes lit up. "Oh, right. You must've asked her about Bruce."

Inwardly, I cringed. It should've occurred to me that the chief could connect me to Bruce and, by extension, Solomon.

"It's a shame she didn't know anything," Naomi said. "I would dearly love to put this investigation to rest."

"I know how you feel," the chief said. "I have a couple of my own open cases that I'd love to close."

Naomi's gaze lingered on me. "I'm sticking around. Can I get you anything? My treat."

"You mean it's a corporate expense."

"Either way, you aren't paying."

There was zero chance of me hanging around to chat with The Corporation's investigator. "Unfortunately, I'm getting mine to go. How long do you plan to stay in Fairhaven?"

"Until I finish my report." Her smile didn't reach her eyes.

Right back at you, lady.

The barista called out my name. I swiped my drink from the counter.

"Maybe we'll run into each other again when you're not so pressed for time."

"Maybe," I said, noncommittal. Fat chance of that.

"I'll walk out with you," the chief offered.

"Have you been helping her with the investigation?" I asked, once we were safely outside and out of Naomi's earshot.

"I answered a few questions. She seemed to think you were an officer in training. I corrected her."

When I released Bruce's spirit from the pearl, he'd promised to take care of The Corporation, so they didn't come banging on my door.

So why was Naomi Smith banging on my door?

This wasn't a question Chief Garcia could answer, so I chose another one. "Speaking of trainees, how's the new recruit working out?"

The chief smiled. "Officer Leo is a breath of fresh air. We're lucky to have him."

"Glad to hear it."

"He's a little green as expected, but his positive attitude more than makes up for his inexperience."

"In other words, he balances you out."

She grunted. "Are you calling me out, Clay?"

"It's not an insult, Chief. As far as I'm concerned, we're two kindred spirits."

She adjusted her hat. "I think I might be a little grumpier than you. Then again, I have a lot more weight on my shoulders."

If she only knew.

She stopped next to her SUV and cast a furtive glance at the coffee shop. "There's something off about that Smith woman."

That got my attention. "What makes you say that?"

"I don't know. I feel like she's hiding something." The chief turned to meet my gaze. "And she was asking too many questions about you, to the point where I had to shut them down. I almost keeled over when you walked in there. I knew she'd pounce."

"I can handle myself, but I appreciate you looking out for me."

The chief narrowed her eyes, scrutinizing me. "Any idea why she's so obsessed with you?"

"I assume because I was the last person at the house on Thoreau Street. She seems to think I interacted with someone called Solomon."

"And Bruce. The woman seemed to think Bruce was alive and that you have information…" Chief Garcia shook her head. "The whole situation is bizarre, and I don't have time to deal with bizarre."

"Full plate again?"

"Between careless accidents and flaring tempers, this town is ready to combust. I had to drive over to Walden Lane at five o'clock this morning because of a domestic dispute. They were both sleep deprived and at each other's throats. I'm trying to shield Officer Leo from most of the mess, so he doesn't have a change of heart and leave us for greener pastures."

"I'd say Fairhaven's pastures are still pretty green, even taking what you said into consideration." I hesitated. "Did the couple mention anything specific about their sleeplessness?"

"Like what?"

"Do they have a newborn? Were they stressed?"

"They were certainly stressed when I got there." She pursed her lips, thinking. "They said they slept like ten hours but woke up feeling irritable. I mean, we've all experienced that on occasion, right?"

Yes, but not all at the same time. I was starting to think West was right. The sleep issue wasn't natural in origin—it was supernatural.

The chief tapped my arm. "Whatever you do, I'd advise you to steer clear of Smith. Whatever her real agenda is, it doesn't seem to have your best interest in mind. Hopefully, she'll slink off into the night and we'll never see her again."

She didn't need to tell me twice. "I appreciate the warning."

"I might give her a ticket. See if it aggravates her enough to leave town. She seems like someone who doesn't respond well to that sort of thing."

My stomach tensed. "I think it's best if you don't antagonize her."

She cocked an eyebrow. "Something you want to share?"

"Like you said, something seems off about her. I'd steer clear."

She cast a glance in the direction of the coffee shop. "You're right. A wide berth is best. See you around, Clay."

I waited a moment to make sure Naomi wasn't following me, then proceeded on foot to the library. The strange sleep issues seemed to coincide with her arrival. She'd identified herself as supernatural, but I was uncertain as to which species. Like me, she was hard to pin down.

But she wasn't like me. Not really. No one was.

CHAPTER 7

The trail of Cheerios on the floor of the library tipped me off to the toddler invasion. Impeccable timing as always. I departed from the trail and turned left toward the adult section, wishing I'd brought noise-canceling headphones to block out the sound of excited children.

Hailey Jones intercepted me halfway to the stacks. "Thank you, Jesus. It's one of my favorite patrons. How can I help you today?" There was a note of desperation in her voice.

"You're trying to avoid the kids, aren't you?"

She grabbed my sleeve. "Help me, Obi-Wan. You're my only hope."

"You're in luck. I could use a librarian's assistance."

Her brown eyes glowed with relief. "Yes! Whatever you need. You want me to read *War and Peace* to you out loud? I'm your girl."

I secretly wondered whether that was a form of torture in one of the circles of hell. I'd have to ask Kane next time I saw him.

"Not necessary. I'm looking for information on types of supernaturals that cause drowsiness."

"Is there a NyQuil demon?" Hailey snickered at her own

joke. "Just kidding. It's an odd request, but I'm sure we can find a few books for you." She marched toward one of the computers and took a sharp left as a small child drunkenly staggered toward her.

"This way," she hissed. "There's another computer at the back."

"If you want to avoid toddler time, why not have someone else work that shift?" I asked, once we were safely at the back of the room.

"Because I'm the face of the library. They expect to see me." She heaved a sigh. "My mother was so good at this. I feel like she's watching over me, and I don't want to let her down."

"You're great at your job, Hailey. Just because your mother was great with little kids doesn't mean you have to be, too. Maybe you're better at helping strange ladies with odd research requests." I gave her an encouraging smile.

"I am pretty good at that, aren't I?" Her fingers skimmed the keyboard, typing at a rate I couldn't hope to duplicate. "I found a few options for you."

I stared at the screen in awe. "You're masterful, Hailey Jones."

She beamed with pride. "I am, aren't I? Eat your heart out, Ida. Right this way."

She tracked down three books and helped me search their indexes.

"I take longer than this in the grocery store, and I know where everything is there," I remarked.

She flipped to a page in the middle of a book. "You have to remember that I basically grew up in this library. I spent as much time here as I did at my own house. I played hide-and-seek in the stacks before I was old enough to read the book spines."

I couldn't imagine what it was like to stay in the same place for so long. "You must be comfortable here."

"That's one word for it. Sometimes I feel like I should've moved away, if only to experience life in another city or town, but you don't fix what isn't broken, right?" She turned to another page. "Not to say Fairhaven is without its problems. It's a flawed place like anywhere else."

"Not as flawed as some places I've lived."

"Is that why you moved here? You thought Fairhaven looked like a Norman Rockwell painting? I wouldn't blame you; it kind of does."

"To be honest, I saw the Castle online. I didn't pay much attention to the town." Mainly because I didn't think I'd find myself a part of it. My intention had been to hole up behind the big gate and shut out the rest of the world. To keep myself safe. Instead, I was standing in the middle of the library, trying to develop a plan to keep the town safe from a mysterious threat. The best laid plans…

Hailey held up the page for me to read. "How about this?"

I scanned the paragraph. "Sandman."

"I know what you're thinking," Hailey jumped in. "Isn't that a television series and a graphic novel? Yes, it is, but the Sandman is actually from European folklore."

Although I knew that already, I let the librarian have her shining moment. "I don't think the Sandman is what I'm looking for."

"Why not? He puts people to sleep and inspires wonderful dreams."

"Exactly. I'm looking for a creature that leaves you feeling exhausted, and you don't recall your dreams."

"I see." Hailey continued searching the book. "What about a night hag?" She shuddered. "Ew. They're not easy on the eye, are they?" She showed me an illustration that depicted a small, furry creature seated on the chest of a woman.

"Night hags induce sleep paralysis. Not quite what I'm looking for either."

Hailey frowned at me. "You knew that off the top of your head?"

"My grandfather was a font of information when it came to myths and legends," I said hurriedly.

She gave me a long look. "Right. I remember you mentioned that before." She closed the book. "I guess we're not looking for a succubus. That would involve more than sleep."

"We're definitely not dealing with a succubus."

Hailey gave me a curious look. "This isn't hypothetical?"

I debated how much information to divulge. Hailey was aware of the supernatural world in greater depth than most human residents. She knew I could communicate with ghosts and that werewolves lived in town. Her grandfather had possessed the Sight, although he'd refused to discuss it with anyone. Hailey even left a protective wreath on the library door; I didn't have the heart to tell her it was a useless gesture.

I lowered my voice. "There seems to be a sleep issue affecting part of the town. People sleep for hours but wake up feeling unrested."

She pulled a face. "Welcome to my entire high school experience."

"There've been accidents and domestic disputes. A handful of werewolves even slept through the full moon."

Her eyes rounded. "Oh. I guess that's bad." She swallowed hard. "And you think there might be a creature to blame? One that sneaks into people's houses at night like some supernatural Santa Claus?"

"Except he takes instead of gives."

"Typical man," Hailey murmured.

"I'd like to figure out what kind of intruder we're dealing with so I can get rid of it."

Hailey set the book on the shelf. "Why you?"

The question caught me off guard. "What do you mean?"

"Have you been affected?"

"No."

"A friend of yours?"

"I've met the werewolves, but I wouldn't describe us as friends."

Hailey smiled. "You're like me."

"In what way?"

"I'm a caretaker of books. You're a caretaker of the town."

I scoffed. "Hardly. I live alone for a reason."

"I'm sure you could fit a few roommates in that big house of yours if you really wanted them."

I shook my head. "Definitely do not want."

"Ask yourself this—why go to all this trouble for a problem that doesn't impact you?"

"Because…" I trailed off, unable to come up with an answer.

"You're the living embodiment of that wreath on the door."

"I'm really not. That wreath has no power, and I have…"

Hailey watched me expectantly. "You have what?"

I buried my nose in the book in my hand. "I appreciate a good night's sleep. I don't want anything to interfere with that."

I was relieved when Hailey dropped the subject. "You and me both," she said. Her gaze drifted in the direction of the entrance. "Is the wreath really pointless?"

I sighed. "Yes, but it looks nice. I'd leave it."

She nodded. "Thanks, I think I will."

Otto Visconti's house was one of the best-preserved historic buildings in Fairhaven, much like the vampire himself. He'd finally returned my call and invited me to pay a visit.

"Good afternoon, Miss Clay. Mr. Visconti is waiting for you in the study."

"Thank you, Heidi."

I wasn't sure what to think of Otto when I first met the cursed vampire. He was something of a pariah in town, mainly because he wanted it that way. The curse had resulted in blindness and an inability to drink human blood, which he seemed to use as an excuse to isolate himself from society. I didn't anticipate the two of us would become chummy, yet here I was, paying the vampire a social call. Voluntarily.

I stood outside the study and listened to the vampire play *Come, Sweet Death* by Bach on the piano. It would be nice to visit and hear *Like A Virgin* or *Shake It Off* for once instead of songs that made me want to bury myself in a dark hole.

I drew a deep breath and waltzed into the room. Otto immediately sensed my presence and stopped playing.

"You're late," he said.

"Got held up in traffic."

"In Fairhaven? I find that difficult to believe."

"It's true. There was an Amish buggy on the road, and it was a no passing lane."

"In that case, you're a saint for holding your temper."

"I've been practicing patience. You're looking well, Otto. I'm digging the ascot. It's very Fred."

He swiveled to face me. "Fred?"

"From *Scooby-Doo*. Never mind."

Otto toyed with the ascot. "My date the other night was with a woman obsessed with the 1920s. I unearthed a handful of old accessories, including this ascot."

"It suits you."

"I'm a vampire. We're evergreen. Every decade suits me."

I smiled. "And so humble about it."

He motioned to the nearby table, where a Scrabble board was set up. "On that note, you should know my game has much improved since our last meeting."

"I expected nothing less. How many times have you made Heidi play with you?"

"Only a few times, but she loves it. She says it's her new favorite game."

I bit back a smile. Poor Heidi was probably sick of forming words by now. "I'm glad you're enjoying it."

He tapped the piano. "Would you like to play something?"

"Nice try."

"Can't blame me, can you?"

Otto was aware that I had perfect pitch, musical talent, and a deep appreciation of classical music. What he didn't know, and I wouldn't explain, was the reason I refused to indulge my interest. It was too personal and too painful.

He joined me at the small table. "I requested blackened salmon, sweet potato, and garlic spinach for lunch. I hope that's acceptable."

"It's food; it's therefore acceptable." I wasn't a fussy eater. I loved food in most of its forms.

"I thought as much." His fingers skimmed the Braille tiles in front of him, and his mouth twitched.

"Don't smile," I advised. "It's a tell."

"This isn't poker."

"No, but you should try to keep your face blank." I gasped. "You have the blank tile, don't you?"

His face scrunched in consternation. "Am I that obvious?"

"It's my favorite, too." I placed my word on the board and awaited his admiration. "Cloud. Double word score."

He touched each tile in order.

"What are you doing?" I asked.

"Making sure you didn't cheat. You could put any tiles you want there, and I won't know unless I check."

"Or unless you trust me. Haven't I proven myself to you yet?"

Otto shrugged. "I have issues with women. Sue me." He added an 's' to cloud and then completed his word—sword.

"I believe this means I get your double word score as well as my own."

Well, damn. "You don't have to look so pleased with yourself. It isn't like you cured cancer." I passed him the bag to select more tiles. "Tell me more about this date. Will there be a second?"

"Her name is Francine."

"Job?"

"Historian."

"Huh."

His eyebrows drew together. "What?"

"Nothing."

"You said 'huh.' That sounds like something."

"I don't see you with a Francine. That's all."

He laughed. "You're basing our compatibility on her name?"

"Is she human? She sounds human with a name like that."

"She's half. Her father was a mage."

"Is she local?"

"Yes. Why the inquisition?" He set his tiles on the board, using one of my letters.

"You don't have the best track record with dating. I'm just trying to be helpful."

"Funny. Your version of helpful is my version of critical. I had a mother, and I'm not auditioning for a second one."

"Ouch." I clutched my chest. "That's way harsh, Otto."

"How's our mutual friend, Mr. Sullivan?"

I leaned back and folded my arms. "Stop right there. We're not playing this game."

"I thought you liked Scrabble."

"You know perfectly well I'm not talking about Scrabble."

He allowed himself a tiny smile. "You two seem to be getting on famously. I thought there might be something to report."

"The only thing to report is that his bachelor pad has enough expensive artwork to pass for a funky museum."

His brow lifted. "You were in his home?"

"Only for a conversation."

"Yes, of course. A conversation."

"You're lucky you didn't put air quotes around that word, or I would've jumped across the table to throttle you." I resumed looking at my tiles. "If you must know, I was there during a rather noisy Halloween party, and I needed to be heard."

"I get the sense that need for you is constant."

"Funny." I put down my tiles. "Your turn."

"You're not going to tell me the word?"

"Why bother? You're going to check it anyway."

He made a show of keeping his hands on the table. "Despite my teasing tone, I do worry."

"About what?"

"About your relationship."

"There is no relationship. He owns a nightclub where a lot of supernaturals frequent. Sometimes I go there when I need information since he seems willing to share it with me."

"Yes, curious, isn't it?"

"What is?"

"That he's willing to share it. Kane Sullivan is a prince of hell. He doesn't need to share anything with anyone, yet he chooses to be generous with you, a complete stranger."

"You're generous with me."

"I'm a vampire hermit. I like the company. Sullivan is a more social creature and can surround himself with whomever he desires." He paused. "It seems to me he desires you."

"You're reading too much into it. He tolerates me. That's all."

"If you say so."

"I didn't move here to find Prince Charming. I moved here to be alone."

Otto selected more tiles from the bag. "Yes, I can see you're very committed to it."

"I'm glaring at you, just so you know."

"No need to tell me. I can sense it."

"Either way, he's a demon and a prince of hell. I'd be a fool to get involved." And Pops didn't raise me to be a fool.

"We should have dinner this week. I'll have Heidi add it to my calendar."

"Can't. I have to do a thing, and I don't know when."

Otto grunted a laugh. "How descriptive and detailed."

"I don't have the information at this point. I'll find out soon though."

He folded his hands on the table. "I require more context."

"I don't know enough to explain fully." Nor did I want to. You might as well ask me to explain the stock market.

"Don't play dumb with me, Lorelei. That act might work on Chief Garcia and others, but it doesn't fool me."

"I'm not playing dumb. I'm too lazy to say all the words required. My tongue gets tired."

The cursed vampire fixed me with a stony stare. "I might not be able to see you, but I know you can see this face."

"Very no nonsense." I exhaled and out spilled the agreement to act as Dusty's proxy. I omitted as many key facts as possible, including the mob connection.

"And you say she's currently a swan?"

"Yes."

"Is she at least enjoying your moat?"

"I offered, but she declined."

The vampire chuckled. "I'm curious—why did you say yes?"

"Dusty is Gunther Saxon's sister."

"And? I fail to see the motivation."

Before I moved to Fairhaven, I would've agreed with him.

"I didn't offer to help. They came to my house together and asked for it."

"Like the young man who needed to find his missing sister."

He meant Steven and Ashley Pratt, Nana Pratt's grandchildren. "I guess, but Steven and I made a deal. He fixed my computer, and I found his sister."

Otto placed five tiles on the board. "And the house on Thoreau Street."

I felt my hackles rise. "What about it?"

"You agreed to help Big Boss."

"Right, but I got a moat out of the deal. It isn't like I'm doing these things out of the goodness of my heart."

Otto smirked. "Heaven forfend. Then what are you getting out of the deal to act in the swan's stead?"

"Money. Gun offered to pay me."

"But you would've done it anyway." It wasn't a question.

"Everybody else said no. Dusty's in trouble, and I'm in a position to help."

"In other words, it's a selfless act."

"Did you miss the part where I'm getting paid? I'm also getting self-preservation. A bonus."

Otto cocked his head. "How so?"

"Because Gunther won't assassinate me for not helping his sister."

Otto blew a dismissive breath. "You know the guild won't allow its assassins to operate within the borders of Fairhaven, and I highly doubt the mage would kill you anyway. It sounds like you've become friends."

"Friendly is different from friends. It's not like we hang out for the fun of it. There's always a reason."

He toyed with a Scrabble tile. "And which are we?"

I shifted uncomfortably in the chair. "Why do you need to stick a label on it?"

"Oh, my. You must be delightful to date."

"I don't date."

"That's right. You hide from the world unless, of course, a stranger needs you."

"You're not going to let this go, are you?"

"I don't see why I should. It's entertaining."

"Speaking of entertainment, I had to meet this vampire at his house for lunch. I expected a court jester to pop out during the appetizers. I hate to say it, Otto, but in his solar system, the compound is like Jupiter and our houses are like Mars and Venus."

Otto stiffened. "Compound? Who is this vampire?"

Oh, crap. "Vincenzo Magnarella."

Otto's hand slid off the table to rest on the chair. The movement didn't escape my notice, but I didn't prod him. I'd give him time to organize his thoughts.

"Vincenzo is very dangerous," Otto finally said.

"I'm aware."

"He's part of a criminal organization."

"Noted. Can you tell me something I don't know?"

Otto was silent for an extended minute. "He and I were friends, once upon a time."

Okay, I wasn't expecting that. "Real friends? Like he came over to play chess and you fed him?"

"Yes. Before I was cursed."

"He dumped you after you went blind? What a dick."

"He dumped me after I could no longer drink blood. I don't think the blindness bothered him. As you're aware, my heightened vampire senses bridge that gap."

"Why did it bother him that you couldn't drink blood?"

"He's a purist. Vin believes if you don't drink blood, you no longer qualify as a vampire, and anything other than a vampire is basically a lower life form."

"Still a dick."

Otto smiled. "I appreciate the support, but it isn't necessary. I left him behind a long time ago."

More like Vincenzo left him behind, but it seemed cruel to make the point. "You're better off. Why would you want to associate with someone like him anyway? You'd never know when he might stab you in the back."

"Oh, Vincenzo would stab me in the front and smile as he did it. He can be quite theatrical."

"Any weaknesses?"

Otto's head lifted slightly. "What do you intend to do, Lorelei?"

"I don't know yet, but gathering all the information I can seems like a smart idea."

"If you kill him, you'll put a target on your back, and your front."

"Really? Even if I cut off the head? Is this a hydra situation?"

"No, this is devout loyalty. Think of Vin as more of a cult leader than a crime boss. He inspires dedication and commitment."

"No threats of violence or force?"

"Not among his network. Your friend the swan is different. She's a tool to him, the means to an end."

"What end, though?"

"That I don't know. I suppose that's what you'll have to find out."

I looked at the small vampire. "It can't be good that he has a team dedicated to developing elixirs that mimic the power of the gods."

"I'd say not."

I drummed my fingers on the table. "So, no weaknesses?"

"Of course he has weaknesses. There isn't a being on earth that lacks them."

"But you won't tell me what his are."

"No."

"Because you're still weirdly loyal to him."

"No, because I'm weirdly loyal to you. I don't want to see you hurt."

"You won't."

He frowned. "Is that a blind joke?"

I cringed. "Gods, no. I just mean I won't get hurt."

Otto chuckled. "I was teasing. I knew what you meant."

"Wow. Now I understood why you two were friends. Two dicks in a pod."

His laughter rumbled through the room.

"I'm not planning to kill him," I admitted. "I only want to know what I'm getting myself into." And how to get out of it, if necessary.

"Well, you have friendly relations in high places. That should count for something, even with Vincenzo."

"It didn't help Dusty. Why should it help me?"

Otto smiled demurely. "You should take me with you the next time you go."

"Go where?"

"The Devil's Playground. I'd like to hear live music, and I'd be more inclined to go there with you as my companion."

His vulnerability struck a chord in me. "They don't have it every night, but we can check the schedule."

"Good. I would enjoy that."

I nodded, knowing he would. "Consider it a nonromantic date, assuming I'm not a swan by then."

His face darkened. "There are far worse things than becoming a swan, Lorelei, and I wish none of them for you."

CHAPTER 8

rolled over in bed as my alarm screeched in my ear. "Seven is too early to be anywhere." There were few reasons I needed to be out of bed by six thirty. In London, early rising was rarely required. I'd speak to a ghost in the middle of the night and track the heir with the information I received at my leisure, usually during a mealtime so I could increase the odds of eating. Food was a big motivator for me, mainly because of a distinct lack of it during my teen years.

I cooked a hearty breakfast of bacon and eggs in anticipation of my assessment. I even skipped the coffee in favor of peppermint tea. The sacrifices I made for my friendly relations—and a few extra bucks.

I braved the early morning frost and fired up the truck. The heater took time to start, and I worried that would soon be another expense. Survival mode sucked. One of these days, I'd have enough money to live like Gun and Cam, splurging on items I didn't need simply because I could. Arguably, I'd done that with my inflatable swan, but it only cost me twenty-three dollars. The real luxury would've been the one that lit up in the dark, but that would've been forty bucks. I wasn't that cavalier with cash.

I drove to Magnarella's compound, shivering. If I wanted to be cold, I would've ridden my motorcycle, although it seemed wise to arrive in the vehicle that had already been admitted.

A figure awaited me outside the sprawling compound. He was tall, thin, and bald, and had the kind of face that would've benefitted from facial hair. The purple puffer coat wasn't doing him any favors either.

"I'm Albert Cummings," he said, as I exited the truck. "You must be Lorelei Clay."

"I am. Do you plan to assess me right here?" That would explain the early hour. No one would be likely to see us before sunrise.

Albert laughed. "No, but this place is massive. I thought it was easier to meet you than to explain which door to knock on."

"I don't know. You could make that part of the assessment." I tilted my head. "Is there an intelligence test?"

"No, but I'll be sure to pass along the suggestion. The team is always looking for improvements." He hooked an arm. "Right this way, Miss Clay. This shouldn't take too long and then you can get on with your day." He glanced over his shoulder at me. "Big plans?"

"I have a ceiling to spackle. Does that count?"

He whistled. "Home renovations. I don't envy you."

I followed him around the side of the building to an unmarked door. He was right; I wouldn't have found it without waking up the entire compound first.

"Welcome to the northeast wing." He opened the door and motioned for me to enter.

Vinyl floor. A coffeepot. A mini fridge. Four semi-comfortable chairs. The room looked like a waiting room to a doctor's office. There was none of the marble flooring and expensive artwork that was present in the main part of the house.

"I think you're getting the short end of the stick, Albert.

What's your budget? Because you should at least request a Keurig."

He continued along a corridor and opened the door to an adjacent room. "And this is where the magic happens."

"Good thing you're not my gynecologist or I'd have to punch you."

He switched on the light to reveal another room with a desk, chair, computer, exam table, treadmill, and a variety of medical devices.

"Are you the one preparing the elixir?" I asked.

"Elixir? Why doesn't he bite her?" He turned to gauge my reaction with a ready smile.

"I'm not laughing at that," I informed him.

"Spoilsport. I can see you're going to be fun. Dr. Edmonds makes the elixirs. I'm strictly an aide."

"Edmonds has a doctorate?"

"Officially, it's in pharmacology. Unofficially, it's in potions. Mr. Magnarella hired him last year to work full-time at the compound."

"He must've offered Edmonds a pretty sweet deal."

"Mr. Magnarella is a very generous employer."

"He must be pretty desperate to fine-tune those godly powers. What does he get out of it?"

Albert gave me a pointed look. "If you're trying to get me to divulge information, you're out of luck."

"Do you even know?"

He made a show of locking his lips and tossing the imaginary key over his shoulder.

"Fine. Then at least tell me what the examination involves." According to Dusty, it was more of a basic assessment that I'd experience at the doctor's office. Height. Weight. Blood pressure. Reflexes. I had no reason to believe my experience would be any different.

Albert gestured to the scale. "I need accurate data for the

elixir. The slightest inaccuracy can screw up the dosage and its effect."

"Is that what happened with Dusty? You mismeasured her height and boom! You've got yourself a swan."

Albert raised his chin, indignant. "That had nothing to do with my assessment. Whatever went wrong was the fault of the elixir."

I winked. "I'll be sure to let Dr. Edmonds know you said that."

He typed my height and weight into the computer, then took my blood pressure.

"Excellent stats," he commented.

I batted my eyes at him. "Why, thank you, kind sir."

"Same for the last one. Kaleigh. Her stats were impressive, too."

"Did she have a positive elixir experience or is she a winged helmet in Magnarella's closet?"

He snorted. "I believe she passed. I'm not part of the team's inner circle, but I saw her name mentioned in a report."

"Why aren't you a member of the inner circle?"

"Mr. Magnarella prefers to keep layers between each phase of the process."

"In other words, he's a super secretive control freak."

Albert's smile faded. "Not at all. He believes a holistic approach to business isn't feasible. You end up with too many chefs in the kitchen, so he likes to segregate."

"He likes to segregate so that he's the only one with all the information and, therefore, no one can threaten his position of power."

Albert's face soured. "Has anyone ever told you you're a real Negative Nellie?"

"All the time." My eyes widened when I saw him turn around with a syringe. "Hey, nobody said anything about a blood draw." It was one thing to sign my name in blood on a contract; it was quite another to offer it up for testing.

"It's standard procedure."

I hopped to my feet. "Nope. Sorry. I have a phobia about needles. I'll take my chances that the elixir won't kill me." Although my blood wouldn't reveal my identity, the report would raise more questions than I was willing to answer.

Albert seemed uncertain how to proceed. "You're going to face far worse than a needle if the elixir is successful."

His words gave me pause. "If the elixir works, I'll have the power of a god. How is that worse?"

Albert seemed to recognize his mistake and averted his gaze. "Excuse me. I misspoke," he mumbled.

"I don't think you did. I thought you didn't know anything. What's going to happen if the elixir is successful?"

Albert turned away and set the syringe on the tray. "I meant what I said. I don't know anything for sure."

"But you have a theory." My fingers itched to touch him and slip inside his head, but I couldn't risk it. If Magnarella found out what I could do, I'd be ejected from the event, and Dusty would suffer the consequences. I kept my hands to myself and grasped for straws instead.

"I have a theory that I'll be completing a mission, like rescuing someone from a maze," I blathered. "I assume there's a minotaur in the maze and that's why godly powers are needed. I should pack a spool of thread, too, or maybe a pocket of breadcrumbs."

Albert stared at me. "You seem to have given this a lot of thought."

"Can you blame me? A power-of-the-gods elixir seems like a big deal."

"It is. That's why I signed an NDA. I'm not allowed to discuss my job outside these four walls. It puts a damper on my dating life, let me tell you. Women think my vague responses are code for unemployed."

"Your boss sure does love his contracts."

"His team of lawyers do, too." Albert walked toward me with patches. "Next, I'm going to attach these to your skin and then have you walk on the treadmill. I'll set the pace."

"What about the blood draw? Isn't that a requirement?"

He contemplated me. "Your stats look good so far, and I'm given a certain amount of leeway. I can get around it."

"Are you sure? I don't want to end up chained to a rock with an eagle eating my liver."

Albert's mouth twitched. "Prometheus wasn't a god; he was a Titan."

"No Titans on the elixir menu?"

"Not that I know of."

I waited until he finished attaching the patches and stepped onto the equipment. He started me on even ground at a slow, steady pace. Gradually, he increased both the level and the speed. I made a few noises of complaint along the way and pretended to struggle at a fifteen-percent incline.

"Huh," Albert said, staring at the dashboard.

"Huh, what?"

"I think the treadmill might be glitching. Based on my observations, your heart rate should be higher."

I could fool him, but I couldn't fool the machine, apparently. I tried to keep him focused on the equipment. "How old is the treadmill?"

"Not too old. State of the art, too, like everything Mr. Magnarella owns." He switched it off. "I feel confident you're in decent shape."

I feigned ignorance. "Does the machine think I'm not up to par?"

"Oh, the opposite. It thinks you have the heart and lungs of Superman."

"Did I fail to mention I was born on Krypton?"

Albert smiled. "If you were, I'd propose marriage right here and now. Superman is my idol."

"If the machine thinks I'm superhuman, will that present one of those inaccurate data problems?"

Albert shook his head. "Technically, all supernaturals are superhuman anyway. This part is more for identifying appropriate matches."

"Are you sure about that? Because I wouldn't have pegged Dusty as Zeus appropriate."

"I can't answer that. All I know is that height, weight, and blood pressure need to be correct, or the elixir could kill you. And we don't want that."

No, we certainly didn't. "Will you tell me before I leave if I pass?"

Albert removed the patches from my skin. "You passed."

"Yay me."

This time he didn't smile. "I'll send the report to Mr. Magnarella and Dr. Edmonds."

"You don't seem enthusiastic about it."

His gaze briefly met mine. "Like I said, I've seen some of the reports. They're not all roses and sunshine. Sometimes experiments go awry."

"Aw, Albert. It's sweet of you to be concerned."

"I'm not concerned. Mr. Magnarella would never deliberately harm anyone."

Otto was spot on about the devotion of Magnarella's employees. Could Albert truly be that clueless about his boss's intentions, or did the vampire use some sort of compulsion tactic in addition to the ironclad contracts?

Albert licked his lips, as though choosing his next words carefully. "You don't have to do this even if you pass. You can still opt out at this stage, in case you were wondering."

"Then Dusty would have to find someone else. What's the big deal? I get a pair of wings and my ego gets bruised?" I shrugged. "No permanent damage."

Albert stared at me for a beat. "No," he finally agreed.

"No permanent damage." He offered his hand. "Good luck, Lorelei."

I contemplated the handshake. It might give me valuable insight, except I believed Albert that he wasn't privy to the rest of the process. Still, it might tell me what he saw in the reports.

I clasped his hand and shook, dipping into his mind for a peek. I'd be in and out so fast, he wouldn't know his mind had been violated.

A quick sweep revealed a recurring nightmare that Albert's employment would be terminated, as well as one where he waited for hours at a restaurant for his date Wonder Woman to show, but she never did. Waiting for Gal Godot seemed to trigger all his insecurities. The uncertainty. The discomfort. The rejection. I felt sorry for Albert. He seemed like a nice guy, albeit one who worked for a notorious mobster.

I left the compound feeling uneasy. Despite his devotion to his boss, Albert seemed less than thrilled to pass me along to Dr. Edmonds. Whatever he'd glimpsed in those reports couldn't have been good.

I called Gun on the drive back to the Castle.

"What's the verdict?" he prompted.

"I passed the physical, but so did Dusty, so I'm not sure how much that means."

"Still, that's great news," Gun said. "Next step complete."

"Hey, Gun. I think this might be more dangerous than we thought."

"Why? What did you learn?"

"Nothing concrete." I shared Albert's unease and the vague reference to problematic reports.

"I'm suddenly grateful to be a swan," I heard Dusty say in the background.

"Better than a duck," Gun replied.

"Absolutely," I agreed. "Ducks are dicks."

"Gods, what if they turn you into a duck?" Gun said.

"I don't think there's a god associated with a duck, is there?" Dusty asked.

Gun scoffed. "Are you kidding? There's a god associated with everything on earth. There's probably a god of the waffle iron."

"If there is," Dusty said, "I'd worship them."

"You and me both, sister," I said.

"What's next?" Gun asked.

"As usual, I await the next set of mysterious instructions."

"Then we shall await them with you," Gun replied.

The swan whooped.

CHAPTER 9

I spotted the blackbird as I parked outside the gates of the Castle. I pretended not to notice as I emerged from the truck and started toward home. The bird flew down from the iron finial to intercept me. Black wings stretched and its feathered body smoothly morphed into the striking figure of Kane Sullivan.

I sidestepped the demon. "My shadow is much bigger and better dressed than it has any right to be."

His eyes were colder than the air around us. "You had lunch with Vincenzo Magnarella."

"I did."

"You didn't heed my advice."

I continued walking. "I asked you for information. You gave it. I made a decision."

He didn't seem happy with my response. "You were at his compound early this morning. May I ask why?"

I stopped on the bridge and turned to face him. "May I ask why it's any of your business?"

"Did you spend the night?"

I laughed. "Wow. Ever hear of boundaries, Sullivan?"

He closed the gap between us. "You know what he is."

"An extremely hot vampire with enough money to purchase Manhattan? Yes, I'm aware." I wasn't sure why I felt compelled to press his buttons. Probably because he was so good at pressing mine.

The demon sighed. "He's the poster boy for bad decisions, Miss Clay. Surely, you're intelligent enough to glean that fact."

"Doesn't that mean the bad decisions are his, in which case, you're insulting me?"

"It's an insult either way. Why are you spending time with him?"

"Because he invited me. Why are you stalking me?"

"I wasn't stalking. I happened to be flying overhead in my blackbird form when I recognized your truck at his compound."

"You mean you recognized it because you're stalking me."

"That decrepit machine is impossible to miss. It doesn't exactly blend in with the luxury vehicles on the premises."

I held up a finger. "First, never insult my truck. Gary is very sensitive. Second, let's assume for a second that you're telling the truth about the coincidental nature of your flight. Why does it matter to you?"

"Because he's bad news, Lorelei. Nothing good will come from an association with him, however fleeting."

My muscles uncoiled. "You called me by my first name. That's twice in one week."

He bowed slightly. "A minor slipup. It won't happen again."

"I never said you had to be formal with me. That was your decision. I believe I told you to call me Lorelei."

His eyes glinted with an emotion I couldn't quite discern. "Yes, you did."

We continued to stand on the bridge and stare at each other. Terrific. A standoff between two stubborn supernaturals; that always ended well. I couldn't tell him the truth even if I wanted to or I risked getting Gunther and Dusty in trouble. I had no intention of helping them out of the frying pan and straight into the hellfire.

"You're hiding something from me, Miss Clay. Something important."

"And?"

"And I want to know what it is."

"Why not keep our secrets?"

"Because this isn't the one you arrived with. This is a new one."

His remark caught me off guard. "What makes you say that?"

"Because I… I've gotten to know you. I can tell the difference when… "

I had to admit, I was enjoying his attempt to explain without saying more than he cared to. It was highly entertaining.

"I'm glad this amuses you," he said.

Oops. So much for my poker face.

I folded my arms. "If I haven't told you yet, then I must have a good reason, right?"

"Or you're simply too stubborn to ask for help when you need it."

"I'm fine. Pinky promise."

"I don't want your pinky promise. I want to know that I won't find you decapitated in a creek!" His voice thundered in my ears.

I stared at him. "You're worried about me."

"Of course I'm worried about you. Haven't I made that clear?"

"I thought…" I didn't know what I thought. That he didn't mean it? That it was all a game to him? I lobbed a grenade to break the tension and distract us both from the current topic. "Someone came to see me from The Corporation."

That did the trick. The coldness in his eyes gave way to concern. "What did they want?"

"A minion named Naomi Smith has questions about the report they received from Bruce."

"What did you tell her?"

"Nothing, but she isn't going away. She asked the chief questions, too."

"I thought Bruce said he'd take care of them."

"I'm sure he did his best. The Corporation is a bureaucracy. It's right there in the name. Miss Smith came equipped with a fat file and a red pen."

Kane stuffed his hands in his trouser pockets. "She hasn't been to see me."

"Lucky you."

"No, I mean she would have if my name had been mentioned. It suggests Bruce kept his word to protect us and take the blame."

I considered the possibility. "Then maybe she is here to cross some t's and dot a few i's."

"You should talk to her. Gauge what she knows."

She could tell I was a supernatural and that she couldn't identify the type. That was already more than I wanted to share.

"Invite her to the club for a chat," Kane suggested. "I'll hover in the background and swoop in if her questions become too invasive."

"I'll consider it."

"You might do more harm than good by avoiding her. I find it best to rip off the Band-Aid."

"I'm sure that's a form of torture where you come from."

"The hairier the legs the better."

"Legs? You're letting them off easy down there, Sullivan. No wonder they've put someone else in charge."

He didn't respond to that. "Make the arrangements and

let me know. Choose an afternoon, maybe three o'clock when we're not busy."

"On it." It would be simple enough to contact her. I still had her business card in my handbag.

He turned to leave.

"Hey, Kane."

Slowly, he pivoted to face me. "Yes, Miss Clay?"

"Thank you."

"For what?"

"For giving a shit." I turned and hurried to the front door before he could see my face. My cheeks were hot enough to burn Atlanta to the ground all over again. I had no idea what came over me back there.

"Well, that was an interesting conversation."

I stopped at the front door to see Ray hovering at the far end of the porch. "Eavesdropping again? Don't you have a skill to be mastering?"

"Not on purpose. My hearing is much better now that I'm dead. It takes some getting used to."

"You've been dead for years."

"You know as well as I do that time and space work differently for us."

I unlocked the door. "Is he gone?"

"He's gone. Didn't look happy about it though. Looked like he might want to stay a long while. Maybe even overnight."

I scowled at the ghost. "We're trying to get rid of this Naomi Smith from The Corporation. That means working together."

"Makes sense. You two work well together. My wife and I made a great team, too, once upon a time. I'd wash the dishes and she'd dry. We'd play Motown and dance while we did it. Our system was flawless, except that one time I dropped a serving bowl."

"I bet she wasn't happy about that."

"That's the thing. She had an inner peace that meant no angry outbursts. She danced her way to the pantry for the dustpan and brush and then handed them to me."

"Good woman."

Ray's smile turned wistful. "The best."

"Kane is a demon, though. A prince of hell. He isn't like you or your wife." I stepped into the house and shut the door before he could respond and wrapped myself in cold silence.

My phone rang and, for once, I was grateful for the intrusion. "Weston Davies, as I live and breathe."

"Any luck with our sleep monster?"

"We don't know that it's a monster, but no. Not yet. Did you gather the information I requested?"

"That's why I'm calling. I can text it to you as an attachment."

"Is this your tactful way of avoiding budget duty?"

He chuckled. "To be honest, I forgot about that. I can swing by now if that works for you. I'll bring the sleep log with me."

"I'll be waiting." I hung up the phone and went to the fridge to forage a snack before the werewolf's arrival. Never a dull moment in Fairhaven.

I stared out the kitchen window as I ate a cluster of grapes. Nana Pratt was in the patch, bent over a pumpkin. I was fairly certain she was attempting to roll it. Ray appeared next to her, no doubt offering encouraging words. They were beginning to make a pretty good team, too. Who would've guessed?

The prickling sensation on my arms alerted me to West's arrival. I finished the last grape and tossed the stems in the trashcan on my way to answer the door.

The werewolf wore his trademark T-shirt and jeans. No coat.

"Aren't you chilly in short sleeves?"

He gave me an odd look. "When did you become Aunt Val? Next, you'll hurry me in before I catch my death."

I held open the door in silence. He smirked as he brushed past me.

"Did you have any issues last night?" I asked, heading to the kitchen. It was the only comfortable room in the house apart from my bedroom. One of these days I'd remedy that, but today was not that day.

"The only one staggering around sleepy eyed this morning was Henry, but he went on a bender at Monk's last night."

"I guess that's good news."

"Not for Henry. His hangover is one for the record books."

"How much did he drink?" It took a lot more than a few beers to intoxicate a werewolf. Their systems were designed to withstand the effects of alcohol. I assumed it was a protective measure—the universe didn't want out-of-control werewolves. Nobody did.

"They stopped counting at twenty."

I perched on the edge of the counter. "Why didn't they stop the drinking instead?"

He grimaced. "They found him too entertaining."

"Do I even want to know?"

"There's apparently now a Henry-shaped hole in the men's room door." He paused. "Which the pack will replace, in case you were wondering."

"I wasn't." I knew West would do the right thing. He was as earnest as Kane was... I quickly turned off the thought faucet. The demon should be out of sight, out of mind.

West brandished a sheet of paper. "Here's the log."

I studied the notes. "Huh. Nobody remembers their dreams."

"I noticed that. Think it's relevant?"

"Probably. It's statistically unlikely that they'd all forget. There should be at least one of them who remembers at least a snippet of a dream." But they all described the same experience of a nothingness. It couldn't be a coincidence.

"Does this help you at all?"

"It might. Let me think about it." There were multiple reasons the affected werewolves might not recall their dreams. I could think of several spells, and as many creatures.

"Where are your spreadsheets?" he asked. "Might as well take a look while I'm standing in your kitchen."

I walked over to the computer and logged into my bank account. "It'll take a minute. The Internet is slow, when it works at all."

"It's your location."

"I know, but there's nothing I can do about that." For better or worse, the Castle was mine.

He glanced at the computer. "I take it back. It's the location *and* the museum-grade desktop computer." He tapped the side of the CPU. "How old is this thing?"

"Older than me probably, but it works."

"You'd get faster service at the DMV."

The screen finally changed to the desired page. "There you go!"

West leaned over to examine the contents. "This is your bank account."

"Correct."

"Where's the rest of the money?"

I pointed to a number on the screen. "There."

His eyebrows inched up. "You can't be serious."

"You sound like Nana Pratt." Speaking of the elderly ghost, I hoped she wouldn't be offended by my additional request for help.

"There's no sense in having a budget when you've got no money to spend," he said. "Why on earth did you buy this heap of blue stones if you were that short on cash?"

"Because I have no financial sense, okay? I learned a lot from my grandfather, but Pops skipped over the money lesson." Mainly because we didn't have much of it, and my foster families had even less.

"That amount will maybe last you through the winter, depending on how much heat you use."

"Only enough to keep the pipes from freezing. I'll use the fireplaces and wear layers. It'll be fine. I bet I can go another six months." Assuming nothing major broke between now and then. Goooood luck, Lorelei.

West shook his head. "You like living on the edge, don't you? Because I can't think of another reason you'd subject yourself to this."

"I'm doing a small job now that will help tide me over." I closed the window. "Thanks for your input."

"Let's figure out how much you need to earn on a regular basis to keep living here."

I eyed him closely. "Are you going to give me a lowball number that guarantees failure?"

The question seemed to take him by surprise. "Why would I do that?"

"Because you told me before that you don't want me in Fairhaven."

He rubbed his rugged jawline. "I guess I did say that, didn't I?"

"Have you changed your mind?"

"Not really."

"Okay," I dragged the word out slowly. "Color me confused."

"I'm a complicated guy. What can I say?"

"I say this with the utmost respect, but I think you're a pretty simple one."

He clenched his jaw and sucked the air between his teeth, making a faint whistling sound. "Fine. The bottom line is that you've been more of an asset than a liability, so I'm willing to roll with it, but the minute that changes, so does my attitude."

"Noted." I glanced at the sleep log. "Thanks for stopping by. I think we're done here."

"I'm not trying to be a hard ass, Lorelei."

"No, I can tell you manage without any effort at all." West didn't know who I was, but it was clear his alpha senses told him I was trouble. They'd been telling him since the day I arrived in Fairhaven, and he had no intention of letting me forget it.

West looked at me like he had more to say but decided against it. "You'll let me know if you learn anything about the sleep issue?"

"I said I would. Whatever you may think of me, you should know I keep my promises."

He jerked his chin slightly in acknowledgement. "Talk soon."

"Don't let the door hit you in your hard ass," I muttered.

I watched him leave from the safety of the foyer. Only when he disappeared from view did I let my guard down. I sank onto the bottom step of the staircase and dropped my head in my hands. No matter where I went, someone with influence was always ready to kick me to the curb. It didn't matter to me when I expected to hide in the Castle and not mix and mingle with the locals, but that plan was scuppered the second I made a deal with Steven Pratt to find his missing sister. Obviously, I didn't regret saving Ashley's life. I only wished the ramifications hadn't been so great. Now West's support was more valuable than I cared to admit.

I yanked my coat off the end of the banister and marched out of the house.

"Where are you off to again?" Nana Pratt asked from the front porch. It seemed her pumpkin patch practice was over.

"For a homebody, you sure go out a lot," Ray added.

"You should pick up a few bags of mulch while you're in town," Nana Pratt said. "You can't neglect the outside completely."

Hands balled into fists, I swiveled toward them. "I'm not neglecting anything. I'm doing the best I can under the circumstances. Be quiet now, both of you, until I command otherwise."

I ignored their stunned faces as I continued to the gate at a steady clip. They couldn't call after me even if they wanted to. I'd exerted my power, and there was nothing they could do about it.

CHAPTER 10

Discomfort snaked through my body as I approached the Bridger farmhouse. The last time I set foot on this property, witches died. Although I knew it wasn't my fault, the uneasy feelings lingered.

I drew a cleansing breath and knocked on the door. I half expected Phaedra to greet me with a shotgun the way her mother, Penelope, had. Instead, the interior door swung open, and Phaedra regarded me with mild surprise. I understood the response; I was surprised to be back here too.

"Lorelei, what are you doing here?"

"Hi. Sorry to drop by unannounced."

"Is everything okay?"

"Not entirely. I could use your help."

She opened the exterior door. "Tea? I just made a pot of lemon ginger."

"Sounds perfect." I followed her to the kitchen, blocking the memories that shot to the surface. Phaedra's mother, two aunts, and two sisters had perished in a single night on this very property. Granted, they were responsible for the creature that killed them, as well as the deaths of others, and the attempted murder of Ashley Pratt, but still. It was a lot to revisit.

Phaedra stood at the butcher block countertop and poured the tea. "How've you been?"

"Busier than I'd like. You?"

"Getting used to solitude in what was once a noisy household."

"That can't be easy."

She joined me at the farmhouse table. "I've been thinking of adopting a few cats. Fill the place up."

Painted flowers adorned the teacups. They looked pretty and innocent, like their new owner.

"No hemlock in here, right?" I asked, only half joking.

Her eyebrows drew together. "You saved my life. Why would I hold a grudge?"

"Because of what happened to your family."

"They brought it upon themselves. I don't blame you. I thought I made that clear."

"You did, but I figured you've had time to reflect, and that maybe you decided to direct some of your anger at me."

Her face softened. "There's no anger, Lorelei. Not at you. A little at them." She paused. "Maybe even a little at me, for not taking action sooner. There are days I think I could've prevented what happened. Then I remember what an iron will my mother had, and I laugh at my hubris. She would've killed me before she'd let me get in her way."

I sipped my tea. "I'm sorry."

"It's okay. Not all women are meant to be mothers. I drew an unlucky straw."

So had I, albeit for different reasons.

"The tea is very good," I said. I'd learned to be a polite teenager, each time hopeful that the current household would be mine until I turned eighteen.

"Thank you. I'm fond of ginger. I use it in as many recipes as I do spells."

I tapped on the sides of the teacup. "Speaking of spells…"

She smiled. "I bet you need an upgraded ward, don't you?"

"Well, yes, that's probably true, but not the reason I'm here." I told her about the sleep issues.

"And you're wondering whether a spell could accomplish this?"

"I've considered a few that could, but none of them seem exactly right." Not to mention I had no idea who might be casting it and why.

She contemplated the remaining tea in her cup. "Has there been a rise in nighttime burglaries? Maybe the spell is intended to keep homeowners in a deep sleep, so they don't wake up and catch the intruders."

"I considered that, but to my knowledge, nothing's been taken, and there's been no evidence of a break-in." It would've been a death sentence for the would-be burglar. The pack would've responded with territorial violence.

Phaedra peered at me over the rim of her teacup. "I assume you're not here to ask if I have anything to do with it."

"Not at all. Promise."

She seemed to accept my answer. "I can think of a handful of spells off the top of my head that would have the same effect, but I can't think of a motive."

"All witch magic?"

She shook her head. "Fae and mage, too." She set down her delicate cup. "Have you asked any of them?"

"It doesn't seem like mage magic. That tends to be more personal." Which was one reason they made excellent assassins.

"It could be a glitch. A spell that went awry."

"It's possible."

Phaedra observed me. "But you think unlikely."

I nodded. "If we knew the purpose, it would be easier to

determine the source, but all I've got are a list of cranky, sleep-deprived residents."

"Any humans among them, or are they all supernatural?"

"I'm not one hundred percent certain. Chief Garcia mentioned accidents and domestic disputes triggered by sleep issues. They could all be supernaturals."

"Or those could be human." Phaedra tucked a stray strand of hair behind her ear. "What if it isn't a spell?"

"I've considered that, too. Given the crossroads, the possibilities are too many to tackle on my own."

She smiled. "The crossroads throw a supernatural spanner in the works every time. You never know if some so-called mythical creature has wandered through to wreak havoc."

"Or been summoned."

Her smile evaporated. "Well, we know all about that, don't we?"

My mind latched on to the idea. "What can you tell me about the crossroads?" Phaedra had to be one of the most knowledgeable supernaturals in Fairhaven. Her coven has been here for generations, and the Bridger farm stood here longer than the town itself. According to *A Complete History of Fairhaven*, farmland had been divided and sold off over the years. This farm was all that remained.

"I suspect the crossroads are what drew my coven here in the first place. They sensed the magical energy in Wild Acres. My family kept journals dating back to the first settlement. They chronicled everything, from the failure of the crops to the activity at the crossroads."

"Activity?"

Phaedra looked at me. "They assigned witches to watch over it in order to learn more. Initially, they didn't understand what it was, only that it had power."

"Did you lose any witches to it?"

Her expression turned rueful. "More than one. They

walked through never to return. The witches grew cautious and learned to observe from a safe distance."

"Kane Sullivan says it's a multi-realm crossroads. Does that match your family's information?"

"Oh, definitely. For years, they left offerings to see what might come through to claim them."

"What kind of offerings?"

"They'd vary it. Stones. Food. Plants. After an unfortunate incident involving an angry troll, they decided they'd rather not lure anything through the gateway, so the experiments stopped."

The witches had acted as scientists.

"They harnessed its power to cast spells too. They'd perform rituals in the woods. Eventually, they realized there was enough energy to power a spell from the farm, so they started conjuring them at home instead."

"Which was also safer for them, in case something nasty stumbled through the crossroads," I said.

"Exactly." She eyed me closely. "You seem very interested in the details."

"Because it seems incredible to me that none of the supernaturals in this town think it's wise to assign a guard there. The wolf pack patrols at night, but it isn't the same as a dedicated schedule." Responsibility for the crossroads also didn't belong solely on the Arrowhead pack's shoulders, but I didn't want to stir up trouble between groups.

"The witches stopped posting guards after the troll incident. That was centuries ago. The crossroads also drove one of my ancestors mad," Phaedra said. "She was on guard duty and claimed she could actually see all the roads converge at once." She shook her head sadly. "It proved too much for her."

"Was she psychic?"

Phaedra nodded. "Psychics are like left-handed people in my family. Each generation has at least one. As far as I know, that ancestor was the only one driven crazy by the crossroads though."

"Which one was it in your family?" And why didn't she glimpse her horrible fate before it happened?

"Me," she said simply.

Her answer caught me off guard. "You?"

"I try to keep a lid on them. Don't want to end up insane like my great-great-whoever she was."

"What are your abilities?"

"Mostly premonitions. Visions." She swirled her remaining tea around in the cup. "It's one of the reasons I left Fairhaven. I knew something awful would happen if I was here, which wasn't a shock given my family's activities. I stayed away thinking I could prevent the vision from coming true."

"But then you came back," I prompted gently.

"I came back." She lowered her gaze to the cup. "And they all died except me." Her brow furrowed. "If I'd realized the outcome... I should've stayed away."

The realization hit me. "You thought the vision meant you would be the one to die."

Phaedra pressed her lips together. "I didn't think they would kill me. I assumed one of their schemes would result in my death." She squeezed her eyes closed, as though trying to block the painful memories. "I never expected them to turn on me. Not in a million years. I feel foolish for not seeing them clearly. They showed me who they were over and over, yet I still only saw a fraction of reality."

"They were your family. That connection will inevitably distort reality." I paused. "I'm sorry. I didn't come here to stir up negative feelings."

She composed herself. "No, it's okay. I'm dealing with it. People say time heals all wounds, but it takes more than time. It takes work, which I'm doing."

I didn't pry by asking what kind of work she was doing,

although I was curious. Pops had been dead for years, yet I still found myself grieving his loss, some days more than others. Living in London had been as much about hiding in plain sight as it had been about leaving my old life and its wounds behind me.

"Do you think some kind of sleep monster might've found its way to our realm through the crossroads?" she asked.

"I haven't ruled it out, but again, there's no evidence. Several members of the werewolf pack are affected. They would've scented an intruder."

"What about a spirit? There are plenty that can move through physical space without leaving a trace."

"That's a good point." I probably knew more about spirits than anyone in town. It was a rabbit hole tailor-made for me.

Phaedra offered a wry smile. "It seems like you might've bitten off more than you can chew."

And I hadn't even mentioned Magnarella and his elixir.

I feigned innocence. "Me? That's so unusual. I hardly recognize myself."

She laughed. "I'd be more than happy to research spells, if that would take some of the weight off your shoulders. If there's a spell plaguing residents, I feel like I should know about it."

"You're not the only witch in town, Phaedra."

"No, but I'm a Bridger. We're the oldest witches, which comes with it a sense of responsibility for the people here."

"One more question. Have you ever heard of an elixir that can bestow the power of a god?"

"There are loads of stories in that vein."

"Not stories. I mean an actual elixir being developed right here in Fairhaven by a vampire called Vincenzo Magnarella."

Phaedra winced. "My family always made a point to steer clear of Magnarella. He's poison."

If the formidable Penelope Bridger had avoided the vampire, that was saying something. "I need to drink this elixir sometime this week. If it's going to destroy me from the inside out, I'd like to know sooner rather than later."

"I wish I knew more about it. It sounds fascinating from a magical perspective."

I offered a wry smile. "I don't have the luxury of viewing it with such professional detachment."

"I'm so sorry. I didn't mean to sound insensitive. I would think most people would kill for that elixir."

"I don't actually want the power. I'm doing it to help someone in a bind." I finished my tea and laughed when I noticed the text at the bottom of the empty cup. *Kindly piss off.* "Nice. Very classy."

The witch offered a meek smile. "I've always had an irreverent streak. My family said it would get me into trouble someday, but I think it's actually what ended up saving my life." She picked up the cup to gaze at the inappropriate message. "That, and you."

There was no mistaking the power that pumped through Wild Acres. Even if I weren't supernatural, I'd sense something special about this forest. It was impossible not to. If I'd visited Fairhaven before deciding to move here, I would've known immediately that I didn't want to stay. Stupid Internet. Nobody should be allowed to buy a house online, sight unseen. Where was a paternal system when you needed one?

I sniffed the air, trying to identify the various scents. I wasn't as skilled as a shifter, but I recognized something rotten when I smelled it. Right now, I only smelled evergreen, damp air, and wet leaves. Nothing that suggested recent entry by a sleep monster or spirit.

I left the crossroads and wandered away from the waterfall in the direction of Monk's.

The snap of a twig drew my attention to a nearby copse where a figure moved through the trees. My first thought was werewolf, but the movements were too… human. The figure finally emerged from the trees, revealing a head of reddish-blond hair that glistened in the sunlight. His skin was almost unnaturally pale. If I weren't me, I might mistake him for a ghost—except for the black parka he wore, along with grey sweatpants with a pair of well-worn hiking boots. Ghosts didn't need hiking boots.

He spotted me and offered a friendly wave. "I didn't expect to see anybody out here," he said on the approach.

"I could say the same to you."

He extended a hand. "Leo Kilkenny. Great to meet you."

"Leo as in Officer Leo?"

He broke into a megawatt grin. "My reputation precedes me. Awesome."

My original assessment was spot on. Like Chief Garcia, the new cop was all human. Some bodies were designed for uniforms, and it seemed that the new recruit's was one of them.

"I'm Lorelei Clay." I shook his hand lightly and quickly, careful to avoid any unwanted intrusions. "I live in Blue-beard's Castle."

His whole face changed, like I'd just performed a delightful magic trick. "No kidding? That huge house on the hill with the cool gate and the moat?"

"That's the one."

"Wow. That place is amazing. It's little Leo's dream house. Your kids must be in heaven."

"I don't have kids."

"Oh, well. There's still time. My mom was thirty-eight when she had me." He seemed to realize his mistake. "Oh, shit. I did it again, didn't I? I bet you don't want kids either." He ducked his head. "Chief Garcia warned me to be careful about making assumptions. Lesson not learned, apparently."

"Let me guess—you assumed she was straight."

He cringed. "I may have made a couple comments that

were not well received." His cheeks reddened. "Nothing homophobic or anything like that. I'm not a complete jackhole."

"It's okay. You don't need to explain." Officer Leo was good vibes all around, like a slobbery Labrador. I understood why Chief Garcia had hired him. "And in case you're concerned, I can promise the chief didn't hold whatever you said against you."

He blew out a breath. "That's a relief. She's such a role model. I can tell I'm going to learn a lot from her."

"I bet you will."

"Hey, would you mind if I stopped by your place one day? I'd love to see inside."

My internal alarm bells went off, not because I distrusted Officer Leo, but because I instinctively wanted to protect my space. "Sure," I heard myself say. "Fair warning, though. It's still a work in progress. It sat empty for decades before I bought it."

"Oh, I can imagine. It'll take years to fix up a house like that, but at least you know you're not polishing a turd, no matter what anybody says. The bones are there."

It didn't surprise me to learn that people in Fairhaven thought I was wasting my time and money on the Castle. I entertained the same thoughts.

The young officer seemed to realize his slipup. "I didn't mean to suggest people are gossiping about your house."

I held up a hand. "It's fine. I know it's not a choice most people would make, which is why it was ready for the wrecking ball."

"I think it's cool that you rescued it. Hidden gems like that deserve a second chance. I bet there's even a secret door." He gasped at his own comment. "Please tell me there's a secret door."

"If there is, I haven't discovered it yet."

He performed a happy dance. "Can we look for one when I come over? I'd love to be the one to find it."

I couldn't help but laugh. "We'll see."

He glanced at my shoes. "You wear those to hike? They don't seem comfortable."

I looked down at my monster-kicking boots. "They get the job done."

"So, I hate to admit this because it shows a level of ineptitude that I'd rather wait to reveal to you, but I'm lost, and I would really appreciate if you could point me in the direction of town."

I burst into laughter. "Your secret is safe with me." I pointed behind him. "You were on the right track. If you walk that way and keep a straight line, you'll run straight into Monk's."

"The honky-tonk bar?"

"I don't think they play country music, but yes, the dive bar."

He checked his digital watch. "Hey, will you look at that? It's five o'clock somewhere. Want to join me for a beer?"

His offer caught me off guard. "I'd love to, but I can't."

"Oh, do you not drink? Sorry, I shouldn't have assumed. I'm sure they serve nonalcoholic beverages. Maybe a Diet Coke?" He squeezed his eyes shut. "I should not have assumed diet, should I? That's probably insulting."

"Don't overthink it. The truth is I love a good beer. I can't have a drink because…" How could I explain to the human rookie that I was waiting for a call about drinking an elixir that would grant me the power of a god, and beer might interfere with one of the many potions I'd have in my system?

"Oh, I bet you drove to the hiking trail. Got it. No worries. Another time."

"I'll have beer in the fridge when you stop by the Castle. How about that?"

He offered a lopsided grin. "Beer in a castle? Sounds like

my kind of plan." He pulled out his phone and showed me the screen. "Here's my number."

I typed it into my phone. "I'll text you."

"Cool. This has been great. Very fortuitous. I should hike in my spare time more often."

I pondered him for a moment. "Hey, Leo. Do me a favor and stick to this side of the creek, okay?"

He barked a short laugh. "Oh, you're serious?"

I debated how to proceed. I didn't want to scare him, but I also didn't want him to wander into a demon realm unawares. "Things sometimes happen here that go unexplained, like Area 51 but without the UFOs."

His face grew somber. "I get it. You're worried about me because of what happened to Officer Lindley. That's really kind of you. You don't need to worry, though. Chief Garcia told me the woods around here have a reputation. That's one of the reasons I decided to hike today. I figured the better I get to know the lay of the land, the safer I'll feel."

Officer Leo was too sweet for words. I actually felt a stab of sympathy for him. If he ever encountered a monster in the woods, he didn't stand a chance. He was more curious than wary, a negative trait when it came to supernatural survival.

"It was great meeting you, Lorelei. I'm glad we bumped into each other."

"Good luck finding your way to Monk's. Next time, I recommend breadcrumbs in your pockets."

"I'd be better off with a spool of thread. Too many woodland critters for breadcrumbs."

I nodded my approval. There was hope for Officer Leo yet.

CHAPTER 11

Following Kane's advice, I arranged to meet Naomi Smith at the Devil's Playground so that I had an extra set of eyes and ears nearby. And fists, if need be. I still felt uneasy about the meeting. My fervent hope was that Naomi would simply give up and return to headquarters, but in the end, I agreed with Kane. The longer I stalled, the longer she stayed. It was time to rip off the Band-Aid. I was confident Bruce hadn't mentioned me in his final report to headquarters. It was likely only Solomon's passing reference to me that led Naomi to my doorstep.

Kane positioned himself within earshot behind the bar. I requested that Josie stay out of sight. Then again, knowing Josie, she'd hand Naomi her ass if the situation demanded it. Might be worth the spectacle.

Naomi arrived on time, as I suspected she would, wearing a charcoal suit with spiked red heels. I waved to her from the table, not that it was hard to see me given the club was devoid of patrons at this hour.

Naomi sat in the chair across from me. "This place is quite an unexpected find," she said, admiring the sophisticated decor. "I'm sorry I didn't discover it sooner."

"It's a supernatural hotspot. I thought you'd appreciate the atmosphere."

Her gaze flicked to Kane behind the bar. "I'm already a huge fan." She opened the drinks menu. "I'm not much of a drinker, but I adore some of these cocktail names. Red Hot Martini. Monster Mule. Bloody Mary."

"Bloody Mary isn't…" I waved a hand. "Never mind."

Her gaze snagged on the piano in the corner. "Will there be live music?"

"Not at this hour. The place fills up by midnight, so I thought it would be better to meet here on the early side. Less noise."

"Smart. I'm not above mixing business with pleasure. Makes life more tolerable." She closed the menu. "I'll have a Hell on Wheels."

"Gin or vodka?"

"Do I look like a sorority girl to you?"

"Gin it is. I'll be right back." I pushed back my chair.

"Can't we just signal to the bartender? It isn't like he's busy with other customers." She snapped her fingers at Kane. "Yoo-hoo! Over here, please."

Kane shot me a dark look. Surprise, surprise. The prince of hell didn't enjoy being ordered around.

I could practically feel Kane's animosity from across the room. "I think he might have a hearing problem. I'll get them." I hurried to the counter. "Sorry about that."

"Are you? I get the impression you're rather enjoying it."

"She'd like a Hell on Wheels with gin, and I'd like a Devil May Care on the rocks."

"With salt?" he asked.

I gave him a prim look. "Make mine extra salty."

Kane kept his expression neutral. "That tracks. Do you think she suspects something?"

"Too soon to tell. She likes the club, though. Mess up her drink so she doesn't decide to linger."

Kane scowled. "I have too much integrity."

"You're a demon from hell. How much integrity could you possibly have?"

"I refuse to dignify that with a response." He mixed the ingredients for a Hell on Wheels. Flawlessly. Bastard.

"Is there anything you can't do?" The words slipped out, and I immediately regretted them.

Sure enough, Prince Perfect flashed a set of pearly whites he'd probably stolen from one of his torture victims. "Miss Clay, you flatter me."

"It was an accident. It won't happen again."

His gaze skated to Naomi Smith. "I think you may be worried for nothing. She doesn't seem very dangerous."

"What are you basing that on? Her custom suit?"

"Her haircut."

I frowned. "Are you serious?"

"It's not the kind of hairstyle a fighter wears."

"Just because she can't beat us up doesn't mean she isn't dangerous. One wrong word to her bosses and this town will be crawling with unwanted visitors." The kind that could cause permanent damage.

Kane slid two glasses across the counter to me. "I could slip a memory powder into her drink. Make her forget why she's here."

"Is that something you typically do?"

"Of course not, but desperate times…"

I mulled it over. "I think we'll just end up with another representative from The Corporation. Our best bet is to tell her enough that she goes away, and no one feels the need to come back."

He glanced over my shoulder. "I could seduce her, then break her heart. She won't want to be within ten miles of here ever again."

"I like my plan better."

He clasped his hands over his heart. "Because mine would make you jealous?"

"Because mine is more efficient." I swiped the glasses from the counter and returned to the table.

"That demon is far too attractive to be a bartender," Naomi said, taking an immediate sip of her drink. "At the very least he should be a manager."

I fought the urge to laugh as I resumed a seated position. "How long have you worked for your company?"

She tipped her head back and moaned. "Forever, but it isn't the kind of work you can walk away from."

Her response gave me pause. "The benefits are that good, huh?"

Naomi tilted her head toward me, giving me a long look. "Yes," she finally said. "And the cafeteria has a dedicated Michelin Star chef."

"Wow. That's impressive. Are you based in New York?"

Another long pause followed my question. "And here I thought I was the one asking the questions."

I slurped my drink, elegant lady that I was. "As it happens, I'm in the market for a job, and New York isn't a terrible commute from here."

Naomi leaned forward, now fully invested in the conversation. "What would you say are your specialties?"

"I'm persistent. Dedicated. Once I start a project, I see it through to the end."

"What kind of project?"

"Right now, it's home renovations. Before that I tracked down lost heirs."

"You're multitalented."

"That's one way of describing it." I'd also been called flaky, directionless, and jack-of-all-trades, master of none. "I guess I should know more about The Corporation first." I made a show of pulling out my phone and starting to type. "Let's see what the website has to say."

Naomi plucked the phone from my hand and set it face down on the table. "It wouldn't be helpful. It's a highly exclusive, highly confidential business."

I played dumb. "Like the mob?" I whispered.

Her look of disdain was one for the record books. "Nothing like the mob." Her voice dripped with derision.

"What were the jobs of the employees you lost? Maybe I can replace one of them." I threw in a grimace for good measure. "That was in poor taste, wasn't it? Forget I mentioned it."

Naomi seemed to view me with fresh eyes. "Your house is magnificently large."

"Why? Does the company need to expand? Remote work would be one thing, but I think it might violate a zoning ordinance if I carved out office space. My area is residential only."

Naomi downed her drink and placed the empty glass on the table with dainty finesse. "I ran a background check on you. The only noteworthy fact was your inability to stay in one place. How many schools did you attend before you finally graduated?"

"Why would you do that if you were only speaking to me to close a case?"

"Standard operating procedure. We run background checks on anyone we interview for any reason, no matter how minor."

"Sounds strangely paranoid."

"We're a very thorough organization."

"Which is where you come in."

"Precisely." This smile wasn't like her others. It was razor sharp and predatory, showing its prey what to expect once it had been caught.

Sorry, honey. I had no intention of getting caught.

"On second thought, your business sounds too intense for me. I like a casual vibe, like this place. Maybe the bartender will put in a good word for me with the owner."

"Speaking of the bartender, I'm ready for another." Naomi waved her empty glass in the air. "Bartender!"

Kane leapt over the counter with the grace of a jungle cat and appeared beside the table. "What can I tempt you with now, ladies?"

Naomi's appreciative gaze skated from his face to his broad shoulders. "Oh, you mean the drinks."

He feigned innocence. "Do I?"

"I'll have another Hell on Wheels. The last one was out of this world."

"Excellent choice. You have great taste." He looked at me. "And you, miss?"

At least he didn't call me ma'am. "I'm still working on mine."

He swiveled back toward the bar and strode away.

Naomi eyed his backside. "If I lived here, I'd set up a remote office right at this table for a view like that." She popped open her briefcase and set a thick file on the table with an audible thump. "Why don't we get down to business? The sooner you answer my questions, the sooner I can soak up the ambience."

"And the sooner you can return to headquarters."

"Oh, I'm not in a rush to do that. Fairhaven is really growing on me. Such an interesting town."

"You think? I have to imagine a well-traveled woman like yourself has visited far superior places."

"What makes you think I'm well traveled?"

"You have that air about you. You look like a woman who's seen a thing or two." I had no idea what I was saying at this point, and I harbored severe regrets about this plan.

Naomi opened the file as Kane returned with the drink. "You've seen one city, you've seen them all."

Kane accidentally bumped the table, causing my glass to tip. I instinctively reached for it and kept it from falling. I didn't realize how quickly I must've moved until I felt Naomi's eyes on me.

"Nice reflexes," she remarked with surprise.

"Yeah. I played sports in high school." It was a lame excuse, and we both knew it.

"Soccer?"

"And softball." And volleyball. And track. I had more energy to expend than anyone else my age.

"I bet you were a pitcher."

"I played right field." I could've been a pitcher, but that would've resulted in too much attention. There were limits to how much I could take part without setting off alarm bells. *Dial it down, Lorelei,* Pops would remind me. Be good, but not too good. Participate, but don't end up in the spotlight. It was a tricky balance to maintain. It became even more important after Pops died. At that point, I was alone with my secret.

I still was.

Naomi stared at me. "I'd really like to know what you are. The curiosity is killing me."

I pretended to misunderstand. "Unemployed and in need of cash, which is why I asked about a job."

Naomi moved her drink to the side. "Bruce Huang was a longtime employee of The Corporation. We received a report from him about certain events at the house where he lived on Thoreau Street. As fate would have it, we received the information after his unfortunate death, which made it impossible to ask follow-up questions."

That was a partial lie. Bruce's spirit had appeared at The Corporation's headquarters to tell them he was solely responsible for stealing their corporate treasure as vengeance for imprisoning him. I knew this because I was the one who ordered his spirit to go there, albeit at his request. They'd likely asked questions, and he'd simply refused to answer them. His spirit would've been beyond their reach.

"What more do you need to know? And why ask me?"

"There were certain corporate assets in Mr. Huang's possession when he died. We can't find any trace of them. Given Mr. Shah's untimely death at the same location, and his mention of your name, we thought you might be able to help us."

"I'm sorry. I don't know anything about any assets. Do you mean office equipment?"

Naomi's expression gave nothing away. "No."

"Did you check the house where he lived?"

"I inspected it personally. The new owners were very accommodating."

Thank the gods for that. There was no reason to involve the new owners of the house. The interdimensional bank vault was no longer in its basement.

"I hope you don't mind me asking, but was Mr. Shah's death related to Mr. Huang's?"

Naomi licked her gin-soaked lips. "Between you and me and this delicious cocktail, it seems Mr. Huang took offense to Mr. Shah's corporate oversight and killed him before his own accidental death."

I plastered on my best shocked and appalled face. "Wow. That's high drama for a company. I can't believe I didn't hear about it. This town is rife with gossip." One more nugget that might send Naomi packing quickly.

"It was a great loss to the company. They were both valued employees." She eyed me closely. "Can you think of any reason why Mr. Shah mistook you for an officer in training? It's a very specific claim, isn't it?"

"I have no idea. I'm sorry."

"Can you tell me under what circumstances you met Mr. Shah? His communication doesn't clarify, but it seemed to suggest you were at the house on Thoreau Street."

"I'm relatively new in town, so all the faces are one big blur. Do you have a photo of him?"

Naomi produced a photo of the djinn and placed it on the

table between us. Yep, that was the guy Matilda killed to protect me. That was the problem with befriending Celtic spirits like the Night Mallt who once rode with the Wild Hunt. Their version of helping out a friend was never as basic as baking a casserole; it tended toward the extreme.

"He was tall, right? Maybe six-six?"

"That's right. You remember him then?"

"I do, but I didn't meet him at some house on Thoreau Street. It was in town. Maybe the hardware store, or possibly the coffee shop. I can't recall exactly."

"Any idea why he would refer to you as an officer in training?"

"The only thing I can think of is that I mentioned the chief was looking to hire a new cop. It's possible he misunderstood and thought I meant me. I'm not great at casual conversation, as you might've already guessed. I have social anxiety."

Naomi raised her glass. "Hence the cocktail."

I winced. "Probably not the healthiest coping mechanism."

"I don't mind the method, as long as I get the information required to close this case."

As much as I wanted to believe her, I wasn't sure. "Will you be able to close it if you can't locate the assets he stole?"

"My job is to verify the information in the communications we received." She packed up the contents of the briefcase. "Which I have now officially done."

I didn't let my relief show. There'd be time for a celebratory jig later. "I'm sorry I couldn't be more helpful. It was nice meeting you, though. Safe travels."

She glanced around the club. "I don't think I'll be leaving quite yet. There's too much to explore." She licked her lips at Kane. "Mountains to climb."

I maintained a neutral expression. "How will you manage the time off? Vacation days?"

"Oh, I'll just sit on the report for a few more days. They

have no way of knowing whether it's finished until I submit it." She snapped her fingers at Kane. "Another drink, handsome bartender."

Kane gave her a thumbs-up.

When he turned away, Naomi's hand shot out and gripped my arm with alarming strength. I quickly put up my defenses to avoid an unwanted connection. She yanked me closer to her and hissed in my ear, "Before you go, I'd really like to know what you are."

"And I'd like to know the real identity of Jack the Ripper, but some mysteries aren't destined to be solved." I wrenched my arm away and settled back in my chair. "You should've mentioned you can't hold your liquor. I would've ordered you a Shirley Temple."

Naomi stared at me with an unnerving intensity. "You're neither a witch nor a mage." Her gaze raked over me. "Perhaps a type of demon?"

"Didn't your background check tell you?"

"Obviously not, or I wouldn't be so curious."

I opened my purse for cash. "You said you have what you need from me. I'll leave you to your cocktail."

Naomi held up a thick credit card. "Save your pennies, Lorelei. This is a corporate expense."

I closed my purse and swung the strap over my shoulder. "Enjoy your Michelin Star cafeteria food."

I made my way to the exit without a backward glance. I didn't realize how much her curiosity rankled me until I reached the parking lot and my legs nearly buckled beneath me. Her personal questions had been unexpected and unwelcome.

I sagged against the truck, waiting for my fear to transform into relief. Naomi's work was done here. She'd leave soon and never bother me again.

A shadow fell over me, and I looked up to see Kane's

concerned face looming over me. "Feeling unwell, Miss Clay?" he asked in a silky voice.

"Just collecting myself. Did she see you come out here?"

"No, she went to the restroom. I overheard most of the conversation. Which part unsettled you?"

"It was Solomon's photo," I lied. "I hope this is the end of it."

"Same. I don't want The Corporation anywhere near you or this town again."

"You don't need to worry about me." I turned and unlocked the truck door in an effort to put distance between us. "You might want to send out the real bartender before she gets back to the table. I have a feeling she'll be making you an offer you can't refuse."

"Like your Magnarella?"

Exhaling, I turned to face him. "He isn't *my* Magnarella."

"If you say so. I'll retire to my quarters until she leaves. Now that we have the result we want, it's best I don't engage her in conversation at this point."

"Agreed."

He glanced at the club and back to me. "Miss Clay…"

"Mr. Sullivan." He was close enough now that his musky scent engulfed me. His full lips parted. He looked like he wanted to kiss me. Even worse, I realized that I wanted him to do it.

This was very, very bad.

"Lorelei," he said softly.

"I need to go." I jerked open the truck door and eased inside. It was a good thing my defenses were already up because the result of that lip lock could've been disastrous.

"We make a good team," he said. "It's not the kind of thing I experience very often. Ruling your own circle of hell is a lonely business."

"What about you and Josie?"

"We're a different sort of team."

My mind recollected Ray's earlier comparison to him and his wife. "This is as far as our teamwork can go, Kane," I said, injecting as much meaning into the statement as I could.

"I may be a demon prince, but you have no reason to fear me." His voice was a hoarse whisper.

"I don't fear you, your flaming sword, or your inner beast. Not even a little."

He searched my face for answers. "Then what is it?"

"You're not my type." I nearly choked on the lie. Kane was a bastion of strength, charm, and power—he was everyone's type.

"Now I know you're lying," he said. "I'm everyone's type."

Even our thoughts were in sync. The world was so unfair.

"And so modest," I said aloud. "How does your head fit through the entrance to the club? Did you have it widened to accommodate your ego?"

He didn't smile. He kept his gaze firmly on my face, as though it might crack open at any moment and reveal all my secrets.

"You should go back," I urged. "She'll be looking for you, and we don't want to ruin our plan now. Thanks again for your help."

"You did all the work. I didn't do anything."

"No, but you would have if I'd needed you to."

"Yes, I would've done whatever you needed. Anything at all."

The pounding of my heart threatened to give me away. I slammed the door shut and put the truck in reverse. Only when I turned to join the road did I dare glance in the rearview mirror. The prince of hell was gone.

CHAPTER 12

I stared at my bedroom ceiling. If I dared to look at my phone, I'd probably discover I'd been studying the lines in the ceiling for hours, imagining them as primitive cave drawings. I was an expert storyteller when it came to cracks in plaster; each foster home had its share of small fractures, and I learned to dissociate by losing myself in them. I only knew it was morning now because of the shards of light poking into the room.

My phone vibrated on the bedside table. I glanced at the screen to see a text from my pal Albert.

It was time for Phase 2.

I sent a message to Gun to update him, then I showered and dressed in comfy sweatpants and a loose-fitting T-shirt. Nana Pratt would not approve.

I managed to scarf down Greek yogurt topped with blueberries and slurp down half a cup of tea before the ward activated.

I hurried to the door and was surprised to see Albert on the front porch. I yanked open the door. "What are you doing here?"

"Good morning, sunshine. I'm here to escort you to the lab."

"I assumed I was driving myself. I know how to get to the compound."

"Standard procedure. Sorry, I should've said so in my text."

"I thought your involvement was limited to the assessment. Now you're a chauffeur?"

Albert shrugged. "It's Mr. Magnarella's way of keeping a tight lid on things." He inched to the side to admire the large window. "This place is amazing. I love an old house with original features."

"I'm working on preserving the ones inside, too. They won't all survive, but I'll do my best."

Albert nodded. "Historic preservation is so important."

"I thought you were the science guy."

"I can't have a spot for both? History and science go hand in hand, as far as I'm concerned. The past informs the present in both cases." He checked his watch. "We should go. Dr. Edmonds is expecting you in five minutes."

"What would've happened if I'd been in the shower when you arrived?"

"I would've waited patiently like a gentleman, but I would've been stressed about it."

The right answer. I closed the door behind me and locked it. "How long will this take?"

"Not too long. It's only a patch test."

I strode beside him along the walkway to the bridge. "This is the part where Dusty turned into a swan."

"Yes. That's the reason they do a patch test. You wouldn't want that to happen later."

"I thought you said you don't know what happens later."

"It doesn't take a genius to figure out a swan isn't the outcome anybody wants at any stage in the process."

"That's fair."

We passed through the gate, and he opened the passenger door to a black luxury sedan.

"I don't have to ride in the back like a taxi?"

He paused at the driver's side door. "Only if you want to. I thought you'd rather sit next to me."

"I would." I settled against the plush leather and turned on the seat warmer. Might as well enjoy it while I could.

He started the car. "Are you nervous?"

"Not really. I participated in medical testing when I was younger."

He arched an eyebrow. "As an assistant?"

"As a subject. I was desperate, and it paid well." I'd chosen those experiments carefully, of course. I never allowed anything that might reveal my powers or trigger me into using them.

"Not much has changed then," he remarked good-naturedly.

I was embarrassed to realize he was right.

The car passed through the gates of the compound, past the entrance to his office where I'd had my assessment and stopped outside an unmarked entrance.

"This is as far as I go."

I unchecked my seatbelt. "You're not coming in?"

"Told you. My involvement stops here."

I opened the door. "Thanks for the ride. Will you drive me home when I'm finished?"

"Maybe. It depends."

"On what?"

"On whether you can fly yourself home." He cringed. "Sorry, bad swan joke. Yes, I'll be here. It's like getting your eyes dilated. You need someone to drive you home afterward. Good luck, Lorelei."

"Thanks." I exited the car, sad to leave the warmth and comfort of the leather seat.

The door opened automatically as I approached the

entrance. It was a different style from the others, more clinical and less classy.

A short, stout woman in a blue headscarf and white lab coat met me in the doorway. "Lorelei Clay, yes?"

"Yes."

"I'm Imani. This way, please. Dr. Edmonds is ready for you."

I followed her through the waiting area to an adjacent room that resembled a surgical suite. If a surface wasn't white, it was a reflective metal.

Imani handed me a folded gown. "Put this on and wait there." She pointed to the metal table in the center of the room.

"Is it the kind that ties in the front or the back? I've made that mistake before and, let me tell you, it's plenty embarrassing."

She gazed at me without a flicker of amusement. "It ties in the back."

"Good thing I wore appropriate underwear."

"Leave nothing on, please. Not even your socks."

"In that case, can you crank up the heat a few degrees?"

She turned and left the room without another word, closing the door behind her. I changed into the paper gown and sat on the edge of the table, listening to the crinkling sound of the material as I adjusted my position, reminded once again how much I hated feeling so exposed and vulnerable. I should ask Gun to double his payment. I hadn't taken into account that my bare ass would be stuck to a cold metal table.

Imani returned to the room a few minutes later and proceeded to take my temperature and blood pressure, and then attach a few patches.

"Are you a registered nurse?" I asked.

"No."

"Not much of a talker, are you?"

"I don't get paid to talk, Miss Clay." She switched on a monitor and left the room again.

I swore they kept the thermostat turned down in this room on purpose. Maybe it was part of the test. By the time Dr. Edmonds entered the room, I was shivering.

He was a nondescript middle-aged white man. Average height. Average features. The only notable physical characteristic was the box he carried in his hands. It was shaped like a cube and seemed to have been constructed from white marble.

"Lorelei Clay, I'm Dr. Edmonds. I'll be conducting today's patch test." He set the box on a nearby metal table and popped back the lid to reveal a tube of clear liquid.

"Is that the elixir?"

He pinched the tube between his fingers and held it up with care. "Yes."

"Are all the elixirs clear?"

He glanced at me. "Does it matter?"

"No. I was just curious. I expected a bright green color or something more vibrant."

"You won't be turning into the Hulk today, Miss Clay."

"Well, thanks for crushing a girl's dream."

"Crushing is precisely the problem. The Hulk is too angry. We want you to have more control over your actions." He crossed the room, carrying the tube in his hand like it was constructed of delicate flowers.

I stared at the elixir. "What happens now?"

"You need to drink the test batch. It's a smaller quantity, so the effects will be minimal, but I'll be able to gauge whether the proportions are correct."

"If the proportions were incorrect for Dusty, why not adjust them and try again?"

"Dusty's was one possible outcome of many. Unfortunately, in her case, it was a result that couldn't be tweaked. If I had adjusted the proportions, she simply would've turned into a bigger, more powerful swan. The elixir simply wasn't a suitable fit for her, which means the patch test was effective."

"How many failures do you get?"

"Far more than we'd like, which is why the requirements are fairly stringent. No humans, for example. Their bodies couldn't cope with the changes."

"Bruce Banner did okay."

Dr. Edmonds offered the hint of a smile. "That's arguable." He dangled the tube in front of me. "Open wide."

"You don't need to strap me down in case I turn violent?"

"You're rather fixated on this Hulk idea, aren't you?"

"It's your safety I'm thinking of. I don't want to live with the guilt of breaking your nose." Although it might actually do him a favor and give his face some much-needed character.

"This room is rigged with special features that would protect me and the equipment in the event of an unforeseen glitch. To date, the worst situation we've encountered is a Bacchus elixir that turned a subject's blood into wine. A very messy affair."

I focused on the tube. "And which elixir am I getting?"

"I don't share that information beforehand. I feel it compromises the experiment."

"How so? It isn't like the power of suggestion can turn me into a swan."

He scratched his cheek. "Are you always this inquisitive?"

"Yes, and also stubborn. You might want to note that in my chart."

He nodded. "You're going to do well. If I were a betting man, I'd put money on you."

"That I'll ace the patch test?"

"That and more." He tapped my cheek. "Bottoms up."

I sniffed the contents of the vial. "It smells like black licorice." I detested black licorice. Given a choice between cat vomit and black licorice, I'd hesitate.

"The taste depends on the elixir. I had someone in here last week who said hers tasted minty fresh."

"Do you remember which god's elixir it was?"

His brow furrowed. "Why?"

"Because I'm curious which god is associated with dental hygiene."

"It was Dantakali. Do you know who that is?"

"Feminine divinity of Hinduism."

He looked at me with a mixture of respect and newfound appreciation. "Very good, Miss Clay."

"What's the point of all this? If Dusty had inherited some of Zeus's more powerful abilities, what would you have done with her?"

"If you pass the patch test, you'll find out."

"It doesn't seem like a good idea."

He jiggled the liquid in the tube. "To do a patch test?"

"To mess with the power of the gods. Remember what happened to poor Prometheus when he introduced humans to fire? The gods were none too happy with him."

Dr. Edmonds pinned me with his ordinary eyes. "And yet look what humans have managed to accomplish since that fateful day. I'd argue it was a price worth paying."

"Tell that to Prometheus and his liver." I parted my lips and swallowed the small amount of liquid. "How long will it take to kick in?"

He checked his watch. "Based on your data, it should be less than sixty seconds."

I was both anxious and curious to see what the patch test would do.

"How do you feel?" he prompted.

I focused inward. "My heartbeat seems a little faster."

He glanced at the monitor. "Yes, I can see that."

My head started to throb. Instinctively, I closed my eyes to block the pain. An image formed in my mind's eye—a large stage surrounded by seats. A stadium of some sort. Was it a rock concert?

Bright lights blinded me as thunderous applause nearly split my head in two. Wherever this was, I wasn't simply present.

I was onstage.

I tried to get a better sense of my surroundings, but there was too much happening around me. People filled the seats. They were rowdy and unsettled, hungry for what I was about to give them.

What was I about to give them?

I didn't see any instruments, not that I'd sing or play music in public—unless I'd inherited the power of a god like Apollo. But what kind of audience would want to watch me play a lyre in the style of the ancient gods? It seemed too niche.

The image faded and the headache eased. I opened my eyes to find Dr. Edmonds' face about two inches from mine.

"What happened, Miss Clay?"

My mouth felt like it had been stuffed with cotton balls. "I had a vision."

"Excellent."

"Is that what you intended?"

"It was one of the anticipated outcomes. Your elixir was imbued with the power of Freyja."

"The Nordic goddess?"

"That's correct."

Freyja could predict the future thanks to her prophetic visions. "The elixir granted me the power of prophecy."

Dr. Edmonds smiled with satisfaction. "So it seems."

I lucked out. Freyja was also the goddess of fertility. I hated to think what that might have entailed.

He picked up a tablet from the counter. "Can you describe the vision in more detail?"

"There was an enormous room crammed with people, like a stadium."

He typed as I spoke. "What else?"

"I was there. I think I was a performer."

"I see. And were there any other performers?"

I tried to remember the images. "I'm not sure. Should there have been?"

He glanced at me. "Did you do anything on this stage?"

I debated how forthcoming to be. It wasn't as though Dr. Edmonds could read my mind to know whether I was telling the truth. In the end, I decided to share what I saw. It didn't seem too problematic.

"Thank you, Miss Clay. This is all very encouraging."

"Glad to hear it. Did I pass?" More importantly, was Dusty off the hook?

He patted my shoulder. "You passed."

I was torn between relief and apprehension. "Now what?"

"Now you get to participate in the final phase."

"You realize that sounds off-putting, don't you?"

"Phase 3?"

"Better. What will I have to do? Bring rain to break a drought? Inspire artists?"

Dr. Edmonds looked at me with pity. "Nothing as lofty as that. Are you familiar with MMA fighting?"

"They compete like boxers but with martial arts moves."

"MMA is a more versatile sport than boxing. It's full-contact combat where the fighters are permitted to use a variety of techniques and skills adopted from other sports."

"Except we'll be using the technique and skills of our elixir-given god."

This smile brightened his otherwise dull face. "Yes."

I glanced at the empty tube. "This is all for entertainment."

"And science. That's the beauty of my arrangement with

Mr. Magnarella. We each get something valuable out of the experience."

Unease spread through my limbs. "That's all I have to do? One god fight and then I'm finished?"

"That's it."

I didn't want to hurt anybody, nor did I want anybody to hurt me.

"We try to evenly match the participants if that's a concern. We wouldn't give your opponent Athena and you Hephaestus, for example."

"How thoughtful."

"You disapprove."

"I think there's a lot more good you could do in the world with an elixir like this. It seems a shame to waste it on entertaining a bunch of losers for profit."

Dr. Edmonds scrutinized me. "You and I are in agreement on that score."

I sighed, resigned to see this farce through for Dusty's sake, as well as my bank account's. "How does it work?"

"When the time comes, you'll drink the elixir and then be escorted directly to the ring. You should feel the changes begin at the sound of bell that signals the start of the match."

"Then I won't know which god's abilities I've acquired until I'm on the mat?"

"Correct. We find it levels the playing field if neither participant knows in advance."

"Unless they study all the potential gods between the patch test and the fight."

"You and I both know that would take far more time than the participants have."

Unless you had a grandfather who instilled that knowledge in you from a young age. "What if I get someone like Apollo? I can't exactly play the lyre until my opponent drops dead of boredom."

His mouth quirked. "Try to retain your sense of humor. The crowd will eat it up. If you can get them to cheer for you, it'll help boost your confidence."

A lack of self-esteem generally wasn't one of my issues. Of course, without knowing which deity I'd be up against, I had to admit my confidence was beginning to wane.

"Imani will be with you in a moment to remove your patches." Dr. Edmonds exited the room with his tablet, no doubt eager to share the positive results with his boss.

The doctor's revelation disturbed me on multiple levels. A god fight seemed like a very bad idea. Dusty turning into a swan was the best thing that could've happened to her.

The door opened, and Imani returned to the room. "Congratulations. I understand you passed."

"Lucky me. I might get to poke someone in the ass with Poseidon's trident. Are you here to tell me the details?"

She switched off the monitor and approached me. "You're to arrive at an undisclosed location at the date and time assigned to you. Be sure to eat healthy and not perform any strenuous activities between now and then."

"If it's an undisclosed location and an unknown date and time, how am I supposed to know when and where to go?"

She peeled off my patches. "We'll send you advance notice and a driver to collect you. It's typical to expect a text within the week."

"It sounds like it won't be the same elixir I drank today."

"No, Dr. Edmonds chooses for you based on the previous assessment and today's patch test."

"Weird question—has anyone ever been given an elixir for Dantakali?"

Her eyes narrowed. "As a matter of fact, yes. Why do you ask?"

"Because I'm trying to picture the goddess in an MMA-style fight. It isn't going well."

She lowered her voice. "To be fair, it wasn't Dr. Edmonds' best work."

"Did she win?"

Her expression soured. "No."

"Because she couldn't figure out her abilities fast enough?"

"More or less. The obscure ones are always tricky for the fighters. I'll leave you to get changed now."

I dressed quickly, not wanting to remain here a second longer than necessary. I tossed my gown into the trashcan and hurried to the exit.

True to his word, Albert waited outside. "I heard you passed."

"I did."

He opened the passenger door. "I'm sorry."

I returned to the warmth and comfort of the seat. "I thought you said you didn't know what came next."

"I lied." He walked around to the driver's side and sat beside me. "I used to be more upfront, but my honesty became a liability, so Mr. Magnarella advised me to use more discretion."

"You're a good liar."

"I don't consider that a compliment."

"Are you the one who picks me up for the fight?"

"Guilty." He did a three-point turn to leave the compound.

"What's to stop me from dodging the fight?"

"The contract you signed. It also prevents you from talking about it."

"I read the provisions. I don't recall any of that."

"It's there. Trust me. You don't want to violate the contract. Mr. Magnarella excels in the legal area."

No doubt.

"I'm sorry I misled you," he said, as we passed through the compound gates to the road.

"Do you apologize to all the participants?"

He hesitated. "No."

"Then why me?"

"Honestly, I don't know. You seem different somehow. Maybe because you took your friend's place, whereas the others…"

I arched an eyebrow. "You think the others deserve this fate because they were desperate enough to piss off your boss in some capacity? You might want to mull it over, Albert, because it doesn't reflect well on you."

We drove in silence until Albert reached the Castle. I vacated the car without a backward glance.

It was days like this that I was glad Pops was no longer on this plane. I was in for a penny, and now I was in for a pound of flesh.

CHAPTER 13

On my way across the bridge, I caught sight of Nana Pratt lurking by her headstone. I hadn't yet released them from my command of silence. I knew there'd be questions when I did, and I wasn't ready to answer them. On the other hand, I'd made my bed. Maybe it was time to lie in it.

I abandoned the front porch and made my way to the cemetery. "I command you to speak," I said.

Nana Pratt glowered at me in stony silence.

"You can talk now."

She folded her arms. "I realize that. Maybe I don't want to."

"I'm sorry I silenced you. I was having a bad day. I shouldn't have taken it out on you."

"How did you control us like that? I didn't realize that was a ghost whisperer ability."

"Because it isn't. It's a Lorelei ability."

"Well, don't use it again on me. I didn't enjoy it."

"I can't promise I'll never do it again, but I'll only do it if absolutely necessary, not because I'm grumpy."

She considered me. "You should find Ray. He was moping

around the pumpkin patch earlier looking sadder than those daisies you left at my grave."

I glanced at the shriveled flowers. "They didn't last very long, did they?"

"Like I told you, next time choose gladiolus."

I left Nana Pratt in the cemetery and went in search of Ray. I found him with the scarecrow, attempting to adjust Buddy's stuffing. Typical Ray, always trying to make himself useful.

"I command you to speak."

Ray tossed me a glance and continued working on the stuffing.

"I'm sorry, Ray. I shouldn't have abused my power like that."

"No, you shouldn't have. It was a violation of my bodily autonomy. We respect the boundaries you set for the house … most of the time. We may not have a house of our own, but we expect the same level of respect in return."

"Like I told Nana Pratt, it won't happen again unless absolutely necessary. I won't do it for petty reasons."

Ray patted the scarecrow's shirt and turned to face me. "I'm going to move Buddy to the area in front of the cemetery. Birds are starting to flock to the moat, and I doubt you want it to become the local watering hole."

"That's all you've got to say about the incident?"

He sighed. "I don't know who you are or what you're capable of, but I do know this—you're a good person, Lorelei. You have nothing to be ashamed of and no reason to hide. Look at your friend Sullivan. He's proud to be a prince of hell. He doesn't pretend to be somebody else."

"I'm not pretending."

Ray gave me a pointed look. "But you *are* hiding. It doesn't take a genius to see that much."

"My grandfather dedicated his life to protecting me. I'm not going to screw it up now."

"Protect you from what? If you're as powerful as you seem, I'm not sure what or who you need protection from."

"I can't talk about it."

"Can't or won't?"

"I'm sorry, Ray. I've said as much as I'm willing to." I turned toward the house and walked straight into Nana Pratt.

"Lorelei, a handsome young man is here." She sounded surprisingly breathless for someone without working lungs.

My skin tingled as the handsome young visitor activated the ward. "You don't recognize him?"

"No."

I rounded the house to see Officer Leo leaning over the side of the bridge to admire the moat. He was out of uniform, wearing black sweatpants and a Notre Dame T-shirt. Sweat pebbled his forehead.

"Officer Leo, what a surprise."

He grinned at me. "I'm sorry. I know I should've called first, but I didn't intend to stop here. I went for a run and when I saw your place, I turned and jogged straight through the gate."

"He looks thirsty," Nana Pratt whispered, appearing to forget he couldn't hear her. "Offer him a drink."

"Would you like a glass of water?" I asked.

He used the bottom of his T-shirt to wipe the sweat from his face. "If you don't mind, that'd be great."

"May we join you?" Nana Pratt asked. Her question was injected with so much hope, I couldn't bear to refuse her.

He followed me into the house, along with the two ghosts.

"Holy guacamole, this place is incredible." Officer Leo looked like a kid in a candy store as he wandered from room to room with eyes like jumbo lollipops. "You're like a witch living alone like this, away from civilization."

I bristled. "I am nothing like a witch."

He gave me a lopsided grin. "Not a fan, huh?"

For a moment, I forgot he was human. Then it occurred to

me that he meant the witches from Disney movies and fairy tales.

I made a quick recovery. "No warts on this nose," I joked.

His attention was drawn to the banister. "This staircase is awesome." He ran his hand along the wood grain.

"Do you know anything about historical houses?"

"Not a thing, but it doesn't mean I can't admire a job well done."

"Isn't he a handsome young man?" Nana Pratt said with a satisfied sigh.

"He is. Dumb as a stump too," Ray remarked.

"What makes you say that?" Nana Pratt asked. "He's an officer of the law. He can't be that stupid."

Ray snorted. "No comment."

Officer Leo investigated each downstairs room like it was a crime scene. I could tell he didn't want to miss the opportunity to discover a hidden room or a trapdoor.

"If you need any help fixing this place up," he said, "say the word, and I'll be here with overalls on. I'd consider it a privilege and an honor."

"I appreciate the attitude. Most people think I'm crazy for investing in this money pit."

"Ignore them. This is a diamond in the rough, and I bet it's getting shinier by the day."

"We're more in the pressurized carbon phase," Ray said.

I glared at the ghost. "Slow and steady wins the race," I replied.

We entered the kitchen, and I poured him a glass of water. He finished it in one long gulp. "Hit me again, bartender. I'm just kidding. I'll get it." He filled the glass with water from the tap. "Can I see upstairs? I promise I won't look at anything you don't want me to see."

"Let him look or he might think you're hiding something illegal," Ray remarked.

The request seemed harmless enough, and I wanted to stay on the good side of the local police. "Sure," I said.

He left the glass on the counter, and we walked upstairs. Officer Leo took the same approach to the upstairs as the downstairs. He gazed at the walls. Examined the woodwork. Bent down to touch the inlay of the hardwood floor. He was undeniably smitten with the Castle. I had to admit, it was fun seeing my house through his eyes.

"No hidden doors." He sounded vaguely disappointed as we returned to the kitchen.

"If I ever find one, you'll be the first to know."

"I'll be dreaming about this place tonight, guaranteed."

His remark prompted me to ask a follow-up question. "Have you noticed anything strange about your dreams lately?"

He took a long drink of the remaining water before answering. "My dreams are always strange. Sometimes I text them to my parents to make them laugh."

"He still texts his mother?" Nana Pratt interrupted. "What a keeper."

I decided to dig a little more. "What about last night's dream? Anything amusing to share?" I was curious as to whether his dreams had been nonexistent lately like so many others.

He scratched the back of his neck. "I don't know if I should tell you. We only just met."

No void then. "I won't hold it against you. Promise."

"You won't think I'm an oddball?"

"We're all oddballs in our way."

"True." He refilled his glass. "I fought a giant anteater. It tried to inhale me with that weird snout thing, but I chased it away."

"A giant anteater. That's a new one. How big are we talking?"

"Size of an elephant."

"How did you chase it away?"

"I dreamed up a bazooka and fired it."

My mouth dropped open. "You conjured one in the middle of the dream?"

"Yep." He grinned proudly. "That's why dreams are awesome. You can make anything you want happen. One time I had a threesome with the hottest twins." He stopped abruptly. "Nope. Wait. That one actually happened. I was just super drunk." He cringed. "Inappropriate. Forget I just said that."

I laughed. "I'm glad you survived the giant anteater."

"I was lucky to survive the threesome. Turns out they both had a weird jealous side."

Nana Pratt looked stricken. "Are there any nice young men left in the world?"

"The dream was a close one, though," he continued. "I must've been thrashing in my bed because I woke up with a red mark on my cheek." He tapped the spot. "It's gone now, I think."

"I don't see it."

"I thought about covering it with makeup. I didn't want Chief Garcia to see it and think I got in a bar brawl."

"Is that the kind of thing you do?"

He grimaced. "I've been in my share of scrapes, but only when it's justified. I'm not pumped so full of testosterone that I can't make good decisions."

"Except when enticed by a pair of temptresses," Nana Pratt mumbled.

"Thanks for the tour, Lorelei. This has been the highlight of my week."

"Glad to hear it."

He set the empty glass in the sink, and we walked outside together. The temperature had crept up to a balmy fifty since this morning. I noticed Ray had managed to relocate Buddy to the front of the cemetery. Officer Leo noticed, too.

"Intruder!" He streaked across the lawn and tackled the figure to the ground. He managed to punch half the straw out of the fabric before he realized it wasn't a person. So much for not being pumped so full of testosterone that he can't make good decisions.

"It's a scarecrow," I yelled.

He shot to his feet and tried to set the scarecrow upright. "Sorry. I didn't notice it earlier. I thought you had a trespasser." Each time he let go of the scarecrow, it would tip over, prompting him to catch it. The whole thing was so comedic that I couldn't bring myself to pitch in.

"Lorelei, this is cruel and unusual punishment, even for you," Ray said.

"I don't want to humiliate him by helping," I whispered.

"Fine. I'll do it." Ray floated across the lawn to the struggling cop and pushed against the scarecrow to keep it from falling. This time, Officer Leo was able to secure it in place. He punched his fist in the air and turned back toward me for validation.

"Good job," I called.

He bowed with a flourish before continuing across the bridge. After the incident with the scarecrow, I was afraid he might fall in. I watched until he passed safely through the gate.

"Do you think he'll be back?" Nana Pratt asked wistfully.

"No clue."

Nana Pratt stared at the horizon. "I think Chief Garcia showed good sense hiring someone like him. Officer Lindley wasn't nearly as pleasant."

Ray blew a dismissive raspberry. "You ladies were too dazzled by his pecs to see he's a few bricks short of a wall."

Nana Pratt gasped. "Bite your tongue, Ray Bauer. I haven't even seen his pecs yet."

He chuckled. "I like the hopefulness of the word 'yet.'"

"You should date him, Lorelei," Nana Pratt said. "He's a

strapping young man with a bright future ahead of him. You'd make gorgeous children together."

"I don't think we're a match," I said. "He's sweet, but not my type."

"Why not date him for a little while, just to be sure?" Nana Pratt urged.

I looked at her. "This is for the sole purpose of seeing him naked, isn't it?"

She recoiled. "That's indecent."

"Oh, come on. You think if I date him, it will give you a chance to ogle him without a shirt."

Ray laughed. "She's got your number, Ingrid."

"He's not much older than my grandson," Nana Pratt objected.

"Try to remember that the next time you drool over him," Ray said.

She huffed and disappeared.

"I think you're on the right page, Lorelei. Leo's a nice kid, but he isn't for you. Someone like you needs a partner with a strong personality, not a sweet one."

I opened the front door to return to the house. "Someone like me needs to be alone."

"You keep saying that, yet people keep showing up at the house like lost puppies who've found their way home." He shrugged. "I hate to break it to you, but the common denominator isn't the house. It's you."

I glared at him as I entered the house and shut the door behind me. My pocket started to vibrate, and I pulled out my phone. Gun.

"I was planning to update you as soon as I ate." My stomach rumbled on cue.

"I'm not calling about that," he said in a rush. "It's Camryn. She won't wake up."

My fingers tightened around the phone. "She's unconscious?"

"She's breathing and has a steady heartbeat, but I can't wake her no matter what I do."

"Did she take any pills or potions to help her sleep?" As soon as the words left my mouth, I knew what the answer would be. Camryn Sable treated her body like a temple with one exception—she popped Nerds like they were life-sustaining.

"Of course not. I think whatever has been impacting people's sleep has infected her."

It was shortsighted of me not to consider that the threat level might increase. "What's her address?"

"You don't know?"

"Why would I know? I haven't been there."

"That's odd. She really should've invited you over by now."

"I haven't been to your house either."

"Next time I entertain, consider yourself invited. Her address is 32 Alcott Street."

"I'll be right there."

I chose the motorcycle for this particular venture. Alcott Street was only five minutes away, and I felt the need for speed.

Camryn's house was a sleek, modernist building with floor-to-ceiling windows that overlooked an empty field. Her nearest neighbor was a football field away. I wondered whether they knew she was an assassin. Unless they also belonged to the Assassins Guild, I doubted it. The members seemed adept at hiding their occupation to the humans in town. I was far from the only supernatural in Fairhaven with secrets.

Gun opened the door as I approached. The ends of his hair stuck straight up, as though he'd been tugging on them in frustration.

I stopped on the doormat. "Do I need to be cleansed before I enter?"

"She's comatose. I don't think she'll notice."

"I don't want her to freak out if she wakes up and sees me in her house without the shaman treatment."

He tilted his head back and sighed. "Just come in, Lorelei. This is obviously an emergency."

I wiped my feet on the mat and stepped inside. Every surface was white. The floor. The walls. The statues. I half expected to see framed artwork entitled The Great Blizzard or Snowy Owl.

"This feels so sterile," I remarked. I removed my shoes and left them by the door to avoid leaving any traces of dirt on the immaculate white tiles.

"She likes a certain aesthetic." Gunther guided me along a hallway to the master bedroom. "She's in there."

The winter wonderland theme continued in Camryn's bedroom. Her sheets and walls were white, and Cam herself wore a set of white silk pajamas. Her blue hair was now a golden blonde that spilled across the pillow like the sun illuminating a snowy horizon.

"When did she change her hair?"

"Yesterday. The other day Vaughn mentioned he preferred her natural color." He rolled his eyes. "You don't need to say a word. I'm right there with you."

I contemplated her hair. "It is a pretty shade."

"I used a bunch of tarot cards to try to wake her, but magic didn't help."

I wasn't sure what Gun expected me to do. He didn't know my secret. "How can I help?" There. Nice and open ended.

"I don't know. You've got talents in the spiritual realm. I thought you might be able to reach her on the astral plane or something."

It shouldn't have surprised me that an assassin was perceptive. His livelihood and his life depended on it.

"I'll see what I can do."

"Should I stay here in case you need me?" Gun asked.

"Close the door and wait in the other room, if you don't mind."

"Whatever it takes. I just want my cousin operational again. Unconscious Cam is too quiet."

"I'd be more disturbed if she were noisy."

Once Gun shut the door, I set to work. I joined her on the bed and rested my hand on her head. Her temperature seemed normal, not too hot or too cold. I closed my eyes and delved inside. I wasn't met with resistance, which wasn't unusual when the subject was already asleep or unconscious.

I poked and prodded. There was nothing there. No thoughts. No dreams. No nightmares. Her mind was currently a black void.

No need to dwell here; I'd seen enough. I disconnected from her and opened my eyes. Nothing seemed amiss; the bedroom appeared as immaculate as the rest of the house. A stark white dresser faced me from across the room. A soft winter-white blanket that resembled a cloud was draped across the base of the bed.

I swung my legs off the bed and padded around the room to take a closer look at the window. It was closed and locked. I didn't see a trace of evidence to suggest an intruder.

I left the bedroom and joined Gunther in the kitchen. The gleaming white cabinets complemented the Carrara marble countertops. Cam probably didn't need a budget. She seemed able to afford whatever expenses she encountered. I envied her financial freedom. Still, given a choice between all the money in the world and personal freedom, I'd choose personal freedom every time.

Gun offered me a cup of chamomile tea, which I politely declined in favor of a banana.

"This could be an act of revenge by a former target's family," Gun said. "It's uncommon, but not impossible."

"I don't think this has anything to do with the Assassins Guild."

His head jerked toward me. "You have a theory?"

"No, but I have puzzle pieces."

He gestured to the chair across from him. "Explain."

I joined him at the oblong table. "There've been people dealing with sleep issues all week. Car accidents. Werewolves missing the full moon to sleep. Domestic disputes involving cranky, tired couples. Whatever this is, Cam isn't the only victim. She's just the victim that didn't wake up."

Gun sucked in a breath. "Then what do we do?"

"Figure out what's causing it. There's no sign of a break-in, which suggests no one is entering homes at night and force-feeding them potions."

"If there were, I would think the victims would remember that part."

"Her mind is empty. I doubt she'll remember anything helpful when she wakes up."

"I'm glad you said 'when' and not 'if.'"

"No promises," I warned. "I'm just channeling my inner Officer Leo."

Gun frowned. "Who?"

"The new cop. It means I'm being cheerful and optimistic."

"Oh. Got it. I haven't met him yet."

"You should. He's cute."

Gun perked up. "Cute like a baby bunny or cute like we'd want to rut like rabbits?"

"He seems straight, and more like a Labrador than a bunny. Lots of energy and enthusiasm."

Gunther groaned. "Gods, that sounds so appealing. Are you sure he's straight?"

"Never say never."

Amusement glinted in his eyes. "Did he hit on you?"

"I get the sense he doesn't hit on anybody. He just radiates so much appeal that he can have anybody he wants." I met his inquisitive gaze. "And before you ask, no. I don't think he wants me. He was more interested in my house."

"Your house does have a certain charm, like men in need of fixing."

I drummed my fingers on the table. "The absence of dreams is important. I just don't know how to interpret it."

Gun rubbed his forehead. "The timing is terrible. I don't need Cam in dire straits. I have enough to worry about with my sister."

"On that note…"

He nodded. "Yes, tell me everything."

"I passed to the next phase."

He raised his hand for a high-five. "That's great." When I tapped his palm lightly, he added, "Isn't it?"

I told him about the god fight.

"Oh. That sounds terrible. You don't have to be naked in Jell-O, do you?"

"Doesn't sound like it."

"Thank the gods for small favors. Can Dusty and I be there to support you?"

"I have a feeling her presence will be required, in case I fail to fulfill the contract."

"That makes sense." He chewed his lip. "I'm sorry for getting you involved, Lorelei. I should've sucked it up and gone to Kane."

"It's one fight. I'll duke it out with my divine opponent and be on my merry way." I pushed back the chair and stood.

"You're leaving?" Gun looked despondent at the prospect.

"I need to do some research for Cam. Can you stay with her?"

"Not all day. I have to work."

"Can you get someone to take over when you leave? I don't think she should be left alone."

"I can't ask Dusty. She's useless as a swan. I can't ask

Vaughn either. Camryn would kill me if she woke up without makeup and saw her crush sitting there."

"You've got an entire guild at your disposal. They can't all be working today."

He pulled out his phone. "I'll take care of it."

"I'll call you when I know something."

My brain was already whirring by the time I left the house. Dipping into Cam's mind was helpful because it gave me an idea of what the other victims had experienced. No wonder they were exhausted despite a long night in bed. They hadn't experienced REM sleep. That had to be the key to determining the underlying cause. If only Dr. Edmonds hadn't pledged his skills to the highest bidder, he would've been the ideal person to bounce ideas off. As usual, I'd have to figure this one out on my own, which to be fair, was just the way I liked it.

CHAPTER 14

I sat in the kitchen with deep regrets over how quickly I wolfed down a tuna sandwich. Hunger didn't become me, but I had to eat before I could even think about tackling Cam's coma.

As I stared at my empty plate in a food-induced stupor, someone activated the ward. I quickly rinsed the crumbs off my plate and headed to the front door. Although I had yet to meet the woman on the porch, her features were uncannily familiar.

I opened the door to greet my guest. "Hello."

"Hello. You must be Ghost Lady."

This was the moment I'd been dreading ever since Alicia turned up on my doorstep. "Lorelei Clay. You must be Alicia's mother. Renee, right?"

Her glare was sharper than the blade of my throwing knife. "That's right. We need to talk."

I debated whether to summon Ray for this conversation. In the end, I decided to leave him out of it. This was a conversation for the living.

"Won't you come in?" I stepped aside to let her pass and gave the yard a final glance before closing the door. "Can I get you anything? I've been told I have the most expensive blue-berries in the state."

"I'd expect nothing less of a lady in a castle."

Alicia clearly hadn't described my meager snack offerings to her mother. "I can make tea or coffee, or water fresh from the tap."

"Don't go to any trouble. I'm sure you're busy."

I sat at the kitchen table and motioned for her to join me. "Sounds like you're much busier than I am."

"I am, and I'm also exhausted, so I'll cut to the chase. I am not getting a dog, and I don't appreciate you putting ideas like that into my daughter's head. Alicia's impressionable. And stubborn. Now she's going around telling everybody we're getting a Golden Retriever, and she's already named the damn thing." She smacked her hand flat on the table.

"What's the name?"

Renee glared at me. "I think you're missing the point of this conversation."

"Fair enough." I paused. "I only want to make sure she chooses wisely. Nothing too banal like Sparky or Lucky."

"She's too clever for that, but it's a moot point."

"I agree—about the clever part. Alicia mentioned that she spends a lot of time home alone. It sounds like she'd appreciate the company."

"I'm her mother. I'll decide whether we add to our house-hold." She punctuated the remark with a yawn, which she quickly stifled.

"I understand that. It was just a suggestion. She seems like she'd be good with animals."

"We are not getting a dog," she said in a clipped tone. "Case closed. I also don't appreciate you filling her head with nonsense about my father's ghost. That's cruelty, plain and simple."

This topic was slightly trickier. I opted for, "It isn't nonsense."

She gave me a look that would've curdled milk. "Don't play games with me, Miss Clay. I'm not some naive wife on the Upper West Side desperate for reassurance from tea leaves or psychic hot lines. What does it even get you? Alicia doesn't have enough spending money to make this worthwhile for you."

"I don't get paid, and it isn't a schtick. I can communicate with your dad. In fact, he's been helpful since I moved in. He's very handy."

Her nostrils flared. "I don't want you to have any further contact with my daughter. If Alicia shows up on your doorstep again, send her home."

"She's lonely," Ray's voice cut in. I hadn't noticed him enter. "Tell her Alicia is lonely."

I glanced at the older ghost out of the corner of my eye. "She doesn't want to hear it, not from me."

"She's hearing it from her father," Ray said.

"Not when she can't hear you."

Renee leaned on her elbow. "This is not amusing."

I made a face at Ray that said, *See?*

"Tell her she's been working too hard. She looks ready to drop."

"Are you serious? You want me to tell a middle-aged woman she looks tired? Why not just tell her to smile or calm down?"

"I tried that once," Ray admitted. "It didn't end well for me."

Renee snorted. "He tried that once."

"It didn't end well for him," I finished for her.

Her brown eyes widened a fraction. "That's right."

Ray practically danced a jig. "Tell her she stormed out of the house, took my car, and got pulled over by a cop for speeding."

I told her.

Renee was unimpressed. "Alicia could've told you that

story. Lord knows my child does not understand discretion." She raised a finger. "Let the record show I did not get a ticket."

I looked at Ray. "Is there anything you can tell me that Renee knows but Alicia wouldn't?"

"I thought you didn't want to get involved in family drama," Ray said.

"It seems like I don't have a choice since family drama has parked itself in my kitchen."

Renee's eyebrows lifted. "Excuse me?"

"I don't like inserting myself into family dynamics. It's uncomfortable."

"Nobody asked you to befriend Alicia," Renee snapped. "She's a teenager. She should be spending time with kids her own age."

"I totally agree."

Renee yawned again. "I don't know why I'm so tired. I track my sleep every night on my Apple watch, and it said I got a full eight hours."

"There's a sleeping bug going around," I told her.

"Is that like a stomach bug?"

"Pretty much." I couldn't explain the supernatural element because I hadn't yet figured it out myself.

"I thought of something," Ray announced.

"Let's hear it," I said. I wanted this conversation to end, so I could get back to the Camryn crisis.

"I don't think she would've told anybody this story. It was somewhat embarrassing for both of us."

I winced. "Is this a story I want to hear, Ray?"

"Probably not, but we've got you cornered now, so I'm going to make the most of it." He directed his attention to his daughter. "Ask if she remembers the time she showed up at the Fairhaven Inn."

That didn't sound too embarrassing. I repeated the request.

Renee's eyes fluttered closed. I was ready to toss a pillow on the table in case her head pitched forward. "It's a local establishment that's been here for over a century. Anybody could name it."

Ray sighed. "I raised a tough one. Tell her I was there with Maria Altimonte."

"He was there with Maria Altimonte."

Renee clutched the edge of the table. "I never told a soul about that night."

I frowned at Ray. "You didn't have an affair, did you?"

"No, but I was thinking about it. That dinner was a slippery slope."

"He didn't go through with it," Renee said. "When I showed up, he left the restaurant before they even ordered."

"I was mortified," Ray admitted, "but seeing my baby girl walk into that restaurant ready to call my ass onto the carpet..." He shook his head. "It was both the proudest and most embarrassing day of my life."

"Your first mistake was choosing a restaurant in the town where you live," I said.

"Not the point," Renee interrupted. She stared at the empty space in the kitchen. "Is he really right here in this room?"

"He is." I walked over and patted Ray's ghostly head. "Wearing the plaid shirt he was buried in, which he must love because he's free to change his outfit."

"Alicia told me he was wearing it," she murmured.

"I'm sure you have a lot of questions," I said.

Renee turned her chair toward her father. "Let's start with why in the hell are you still here? Why not join Mom in the afterlife? She's probably waiting on you in heaven just like she was always waiting on you here."

I folded my arms. "You see, Ray. This is why I don't involve myself in squabbles."

Ray looked ready to melt into the floorboards, which he could do if he really wanted.

All at once, the fight seemed to leave Renee. Her shoulders sagged and her head lolled to the side. "I can't … seem to keep my eyes open," she whispered.

I dashed toward her and eased her head onto the table to avoid a nasty bump.

Ray gaped at her. "Did she just fall asleep in the middle of an argument?"

I lifted her arm and dropped it. "Yep."

Ray drifted closer to her and peered at her face. "What's going on?"

"I'm not sure. There's been a sleep issue all over town this week. I've been trying to dig into it, but it's been hard with Dusty's issue, plus the investigator from The Corporation."

Ray glanced at me. "Interesting."

"The supernatural world always is."

"No, I mean this. Your response. You make it sound like it's your job to fix. I think that's interesting for someone who claims to want peace and quiet."

I shrugged. "With great power comes lots of pains in the ass?"

"Isn't it pain in the asses?"

"I don't think so." I crouched beside Renee and jostled her. "Can you hear me?"

She didn't stir.

"Is this normal?" Ray asked.

"Do people normally fall asleep in the middle of heated conversations?" I contemplated her size. "How much does she weigh?"

"She's put on a few pounds since I died. I'd guess one-sixty."

"I think I can manage that."

"Are you sure? That's a lot."

"Do not dare say that when she's awake."

"I can help." Ray moved to the opposite side of the chair and scrunched his face in a tight ball as he focused on shifting his daughter. Her body inched to the left until I was able to get my arms under her.

Ray rushed to my side and supported some of her weight as I lifted her into my arms. I didn't have the heart to tell him I didn't need his help.

"I don't have a bed in the spare bedroom. I'll have to take her to mine," I said.

Ray and I carried her upstairs and placed her in my bed.

"That was impressive poltergeist action, Ray."

"Me? I can't believe you. You don't seem like you could lift more than a heavy box." He studied me. "Why are you so strong?"

"Years of practice," I said vaguely.

"Really? I haven't seen you lift anything heavier than a hammer since you moved in."

I ignored him, choosing to focus on the immediate problem. "I think she's in a coma, like Cam."

"Should we call a doctor?"

"No. I have someone else in mind."

Ray stroked his daughter's hair. "I don't want Alicia to worry. Would you mind if she stays here until Renee wakes up?"

How could I say no? "Fine. Alicia can sleep with her mom. I have a sleeping bag somewhere for me. I'll find it."

"Thank you, Lorelei. I know this isn't ideal."

"Would you give me a minute alone with your daughter? I'd like to try something."

Ray looked skeptical. "It doesn't involve stuffing a pillow over her face, does it?"

I burst into laughter. "Why would I do that?"

"Because you don't want people in your house."

"That's true, but I wouldn't resort to murder to put an end

to my misery. I thought you knew me better than that by now."

"I was only joking." He paused. "Sort of."

"Why don't you go hunt for my sleeping bag? I think it's in one of the other closets."

I waited until he disappeared to sit beside Renee on the bed. I was fairly certain I already knew what I'd find in her head, but I needed confirmation before I made my next move. I placed a hand on her head and closed my eyes.

Her mind was blank.

No dreams. No nightmares. No images of any kind.

I double-checked her breath and pulse. Still good. Same as Cam.

I observed her, debating a couple options. I didn't want to try this next move, but it seemed necessary. I slipped back inside her head and did what I did best.

Conjuring a nightmare was as simple as breathing. I tapped into the fears that lay dormant in her mind and created a story with them.

Unsurprisingly, Renee's greatest fear involved her daughter.

Renee sat behind the wheel of a nondescript SUV with Alicia in the passenger seat. They rode along a scenic pass that reminded me of Route 1 that ran along coastal California. Renee's husband had moved there. Maybe it was connected to him.

Renee lost control of the wheel and was ejected from the vehicle, leaving Alicia trapped inside as it spun toward the edge. Renee screamed, watching helplessly as the SUV teetered on the edge of the cliff with her daughter trapped inside.

I didn't enjoy watching Alicia come to any harm, even when it wasn't real. I intervened, dragging the car back from the cliff so it didn't fall. The passenger door opened, and Alicia spilled to the ground.

Once she was safe on land, I exited the dream.

Renee's eyes remained closed.

I rose to my feet, thinking. I could help her conjure a nightmare, but she wasn't able to create her own. Hmm.

I considered calling Kane for the healer on his payroll at the club. In the end, I opted to contact Sage, the fae healer I met through the wolf pack. Even if she couldn't revive Renee, she might have a sense of what was happening that would help both Renee and Camryn.

Sage was eager to assist me, if only for an insider look at the Castle. Even on the cusp of winter, the cheerful fae showed up in shorts and sandals, albeit with a patchwork sweater. Her blonde hair was streaked with pink, and her youthful face would keep you guessing her age for hours. She spent five minutes in the foyer, staring at each wall, the floor, and then the ceiling.

"Such great vibes," she said in a quiet voice.

"There are even better vibes upstairs. Why don't we go to my room and see?" I paused. "That sounded more appropriate in my head."

I practically pushed her to the staircase.

Like Officer Leo, she paused to admire the woodwork of the banister. "This place is amazing. I can't wait to see how it looks when you're finished fixing it up."

"You'll be dead by then," I quipped.

"Oh, you'd be surprised. We fae can live a long time." She followed me upstairs to the master bedroom where I found Ray standing sentry over his daughter's body.

His brow furrowed at the sight of Sage. "This is the healer?"

"Don't judge a book by its cover, Ray."

Sage's face brightened like a pale star. "Oh, is your ghost here?"

"The ghost is this woman's father, so he has a vested interest in the outcome."

Sage sucked a breath between her teeth. "I'll do my best, sir. No promises. I've heard about this sleep spell going around, but I haven't had a chance to observe it firsthand until now."

"West hasn't asked you to treat the pack?" I asked.

"We spoke about the fatigue, but nobody's unconscious over there that I know of."

"They might be now." I shot off a text to West while Sage set to work. If the people previously affected started to fall into comas, we'd have an even bigger problem on our hands.

Sage opened her canvas tote bag and removed a jar of herbs. "Do you mind if I rub this on her forehead?"

"He's over there." I pointed to the corner where Ray now hovered.

"Do whatever you have to do," Ray said.

"Go for it," I told Sage.

She opened the jar, releasing a mixture of scents I couldn't identify.

"Sea-buckthorn is the primary ingredient," she said, as though anticipating my question. "It's a hex breaker."

"Should we leave?" I asked.

"No, I like company when I work." She frowned. "Except my grandmother. She's my worst critic. I could create the most perfect mixture in the world, and she'd say the lavender had too much purple in it."

I gestured to Renee. "Could we maybe…?"

Sage snapped to attention. "Oh, right. Sorry about that. It can be hard living in such cramped quarters with your loved ones. This house would be paradise for us." She dabbed some of the mixture on Renee's forehead. "Except we'd have more furniture. It seems so bare."

"Well, it's just me, and I'm spending most of my time and money on the renovations right now." And survival. Story of my life.

"I can help you find a sofa for your parlor room, or living

room, whatever you call it. I'm an excellent thrifter." She glanced at her clothing. "I realize this outfit doesn't support my claim. I have pieces I assemble from multiple decades that look like they were designed to be worn together."

"Accept her offer," Ray urged.

I fought the urge to shush him, not for Sage's sake since she couldn't hear him, but for mine.

"That sounds good," I said vaguely.

"Okay, now I need a minute of silence while I focus." Sage concentrated on Renee.

I gazed out the window at the backyard where a flock of birds were pecking the ground. They seemed to have migrated there in light of the scarecrow's relocation to the far side of the property.

"Renee, can you hear me?" Sage asked. "If you can, I need a sign."

She remained motionless on the bed.

"Can you move a finger?" Sage asked. "One little pinky?"

Nothing happened.

"Let me try a different blend." She reached into the tote bag and produced a second jar. This one was more colorful and when she opened the lid, a honey-sweet fragrance hit me in the face.

"Echinacea?" I asked.

"Yes, and blackthorn and blessed thistle," Sage said. She used a cloth to wipe away the first mixture and applied the second, followed by the same questions to Renee but to no avail.

"I haven't seen any movement, have you?" I asked.

Sage regarded the patient. "No. This is bad."

"Did you invite her here to state the obvious?" Ray asked, unusually agitated.

"Did you learn anything at all?" I asked.

Sage nodded. "It isn't a spell."

"Really? You're sure?" I couldn't decide if that was good news or bad news.

"It's supernatural but not magical." She rummaged through the tote bag and produced a potion bottle. "I'm going to leave this for you. It will help keep her nourished and her system functional, so her body doesn't start shutting down. One teaspoon per day. Hopefully, you'll be able to wake her up before you've used it all."

"Would you mind dropping off a bottle at Camryn Sable's house? She's currently in the same condition."

Sage's eyes widened. "It's an epidemic."

"It might become one soon if we don't stop it." No pressure, Lorelei. "I appreciate you coming over on such short notice. What do I owe you?"

"Are you kidding? I would've dropped anything to see the inside of this place." She glanced at Renee. "And to help someone in need, of course. I'm only sorry I couldn't do more."

"If you hear about anyone else in this situation, will you let me know?"

"Of course. Wow. I hope this doesn't become the new normal. A town full of comatose people would make this a very dull place." She hefted the strap of the bag over her shoulder. "Peace out."

Sage left the bedroom, leaving me alone with Renee and Ray. The ghost stared down at his daughter with a forlorn expression that poked my ribcage.

"Why don't I text Alicia now and tell her to bring an overnight bag? That way she'll be here in time for dinner."

"I would appreciate that, Lorelei. Thank you."

I started toward the bedroom doorway.

"I know this is your sanctuary and I don't mean to intrude, but would you mind if I stay with her?"

I thought of Pops and how desperate he would've been to

remain by my side in times of trouble. "Stay with her as long as you want," I said.

"If she doesn't make it," he began, "I want you to make sure she crosses over. Don't let her stick around for Alicia. I know she'll want to."

I glanced at him over my shoulder. "I won't let her stay."

He nodded solemnly. "I knew I could count on you for that."

"I'm not giving up hope, Ray, and neither should you."

He hovered beside his daughter. "I won't. If I abandon hope, then I abandon her."

Unfortunately, I knew that feeling all too well.

CHAPTER 15

"What's wrong with my mom?" Alicia asked. She'd arrived at the Castle with a duffel bag and her school backpack, no questions asked until now. She sat at the kitchen table with a plate dotted with chicken nuggets and a dollop of ketchup in the center.

I glanced at the plate. "Did you design a summoning circle?"

Alicia beamed proudly. "Yep. That's the blood." She pointed to the ketchup. "Do we need to summon someone to help my mom?"

"We're not summoning anyone," I said firmly. "We're trying to help your mom another way. There's some sort of sleep issue going around that seems to have affected her. For now, it's best if the two of you stay here."

Alicia perked up. "Is it a spell like in *Sleeping Beauty* or *Snow White*? Do we need to find a prince to kiss her? Because Prince Harry lives in America now. I bet he'd come if we asked him."

"A spell was one theory, but it's been crossed off the list."

Alicia nibbled thoughtfully on a nugget. "She's been really

sleepy lately. Even when she sleeps all night without getting up twice to pee, she's still been tired."

I cast a sidelong glance at her. "You know how many times she gets up to pee?"

"She complains about it all the time. Believe me, there are some things I'd rather not know."

"Has she visited anywhere unusual lately? Any places she wouldn't typically go?"

Alicia shook her head. "Not that I know of, but she doesn't tell me her schedule, except to say when she'll be home and what to order for dinner."

"Has she been working extra hours?"

"I don't think there are any left to work unless she plans to move into the office and sleep there."

Pain stabbed my chest. I related to Alicia more than she knew. Left alone is left alone, no matter how or why it's accomplished. "I have ice cream if you're interested."

"It's November."

"Do you stop eating fat and sugar in November?"

"Hell no. This stomach is open for business all year round."

I opened the freezer and fetched the carton of ice cream to let it thaw a bit. "Thought so."

"Do you think somebody might've summoned a sleeping demon?" Alicia asked. "Maybe a kid who didn't want to go to school."

I pulled down a bowl from the shelf. "Unlikely."

"But possible, right? If I learned about the crossroads and demons, someone else could have too."

I didn't own an ice cream scooper, so I opted for a serving spoon. "It's possible. Still unlikely."

"Then what do you think happened to my mom, and why didn't it happen to me?" Her brown eyes glistened with unshed tears.

I leaned across the counter to address her closely. "Alicia, I know what you're thinking, and I want you to hear me. This is not your fault. This has nothing to do with the demon you summoned or anything else related to you."

"You don't know that. I read about these hitchhiker demons that attach themselves to the summoned one. What if some crazy coma demon hitchhiked to Fairhaven with the one I called?"

"Then we would've known about it long before now. Too much time has passed since then."

Alicia's gaze dropped to the counter. "You swear?"

"I can't say never, but I can tell you the chances are infinitesimally small." I filled the small bowl with ice cream and slid it to Alicia.

"Got any chocolate syrup?" she asked.

"I don't, but I can throw a few blueberries on top."

She wrinkled her nose. "Thanks, I'll pass."

I watched her dive into the ice cream with gusto.

"Aren't you going to have any?" she asked between mouthfuls.

"I'm not in the mood." My mind was working overtime to figure out exactly how much danger Renee and Cam were in. Alicia's presence in my house only added to the pressure; I refused to let the teenager lose her mother on my watch.

Alicia made short work of the dessert. I was impressed that she brought the bowl to the sink to rinse it without prompting.

"It's getting late, and you have school tomorrow," I said. "You should go upstairs now and get ready for bed."

"Can I watch TV first?"

"You could if I owned one. Now go on up."

"Yes, ma'am." Alicia skirted the island and disappeared through the kitchen doorway.

I unhooked a sweater from the back of a chair and slipped it over my head. Although the air was cool and crisp, it wasn't too cold to linger on the front porch for a few minutes before I turned in. I needed to unwind in solitude.

I stepped onto the porch and closed the door behind me. The lights of downtown Fairhaven glittered below. Even with the bright moon and stars, it was too dark to glimpse the river at the other end of town.

I sat on the step and hugged myself. Alicia's concern that a demon had hitched a ride through the crossroads gnawed at me, not because I secretly believed it was true; my point about timing was valid. And now I couldn't stop thinking about the timing. It bothered me that the town's sleep issues seemed to coincide with the arrival of both The Corporation's investigator and Officer Leo. What if one of them was the cause? Officer Leo was human, though, I was certain of it. And I already knew Naomi wasn't—but neither did she have any reason to put people in comas. Still, I couldn't ignore the timing.

"You shouldn't let the child eat that much sugar before bed," Nana Pratt's voice interrupted my thought spiral.

"Were you spying through the window?" I asked.

"I only wanted to check on Renee."

I gave her a knowing look. "Renee isn't asleep in my kitchen."

"Fine. I don't like drifting that high. I prefer to stay close to the ground. Any higher reminds me I'm a ghost."

"You don't want a reminder?"

"No, I prefer to think of myself as still human."

"That's part of the reason you're still tethered to this plane; you know that, right?"

Nana Pratt curled her lip. "I don't care to continue this conversation. How's Renee?"

"No change. I'm going to get ready for bed and try to get a good night's sleep so I can think better tomorrow."

"It's kind of you to let them sleep upstairs. I can tell it isn't easy for you—letting people in."

"Renee needs help," I said simply.

"Ray is trying not to show it, but I can tell he's on edge," Nana Pratt said.

"I don't blame him. It's horrible to watch someone you love suffer when you know there's nothing you can do to help them."

Nana Pratt regarded me. "Sounds like you have personal experience."

I didn't care to continue this conversation either. I stood and walked back toward the front door. "Ray knows I'm doing everything I can, right?"

"Of course he does."

Satisfied, I opened the door and retreated inside.

Now dressed in a T-shirt and sweatpants, Alicia was waiting for me on the bottom step of the staircase. "What were you doing out there?"

"Collecting my thoughts. Why aren't you in bed?"

"I don't know how I feel about sleeping next to my mom when she's … like that. What if I catch it?"

"I don't think it works that way."

Alicia remained rooted to the step. "What if she wakes up and I'm right next to her? She won't like that. She'll call me a baby for wanting to sleep with her."

"Studies have shown that when someone is in a coma, the voices of family members can increase their level of consciousness. I think it would be good for your mom if she knew on some level that you were right there with her."

Alicia gripped the banister and pulled herself to her feet. "Then I'd be helping her by sleeping next to her."

"Exactly."

"Okay. I'll do that." She started to turn and stopped abruptly. "Where will you sleep?"

"I'm going to unroll my sleeping bag downstairs to give you privacy."

Alicia laughed. "This place is a castle. You could have a squatter living upstairs and not know."

"Fine, I'd like to give myself privacy."

Alicia shrugged. "Suit yourself. Good night, Ghost Lady. Thanks for the ice cream."

"You're welcome."

I brushed my teeth and washed my face in the downstairs bathroom so as not to disturb Alicia. I forgot to grab a pillow, but there was no way I was getting one now, so I rolled up the sweater I'd been wearing and stuffed it underneath my head. Pops hammered into me how necessary it was to be resourceful, that I never knew when I'd find myself in a difficult situation.

If he only knew how many times that advice had come in handy.

It took me a few minutes to get comfortable. Despite the sleeping bag, I could still feel the hardness of the floor beneath me. My back and neck would be sore tomorrow. Good thing I healed quickly.

I closed my eyes and emptied my thoughts. I needed a break from all the challenges I was currently facing. If I could craft a pleasant dream that involved puppies sliding down rainbows, that would be great. It should be simple enough for someone with my skills, but tonight I struggled. In the end, I settled for a relaxing tropical island dream. Reclining in my imaginary lounge chair, I listened to the waves crash against the shore as I sipped a cocktail beneath my oversized sunhat. I had the beach to myself, of course. I preferred a life of solitude even in my dreams.

As the sun warmed my skin, I felt a strange pressure along my sinuses. I set the glass in the sand and rubbed my forehead.

The pressure increased, and then I felt it. An unfamiliar presence.

I was no longer alone on the beach.

I bolted upright. This was *my* dream. There shouldn't have been anything unfamiliar or unwelcome in my headspace. It wasn't possible.

My gaze ran along the shoreline. Nothing unusual there. I turned left and saw only palm trees.

Then I turned right.

The creature resembled a tapir, a primitive animal that people sometimes mistook for a relative of anteaters, except this creature was enormous. Maybe Officer Leo's description of his strange dream had influenced my own. The creature seemed to be trying to suck the sand into its elongated nose and mouth.

Not just the sand, everything in its path. I watched in amazement as it inhaled slick black rocks from a nearby jetty, leaving only sand and water behind.

Despite the tropical sun, my body grew cold. No. There was no way I conjured this creature. What was happening?

I stared at the dream invader, deliberating my next move. If I let it keep sucking, I might disappear along with everything else in my mind.

I vacated the chair, knocking over the cocktail glass in the process. Dammit, that was the perfect paloma.

"I'd stop now if I were you," I told the tapir.

The creature stopped sucking long enough to regard me with interest. I recalled Officer Leo's mention of summoning a bazooka. I didn't think that would be necessary.

"You picked the wrong head tonight, friend."

The creature seemed to sense my power because it did an about-face and ran. I chased after it, uncertain whether it could be killed in a dream, or whether I had to track it down in the external world. I was willing to roll the dice.

The tapir was fast for an awkward chunky giant.

It made a sharp turn and splashed through the gentle waves. I wasn't sure of its intention; it didn't look like much of a swimmer. When it pivoted to face me, I realized its plan.

The creature unleashed all the water it had inhaled through its snout. It was basically like unloading a firehose on a person. I dodged the intense spray and fell on the sand. By the time I recovered my footing, the creature was nowhere to be seen; it had escaped the dream.

There was nothing left to do but wake myself up. Heart pounding, I pulled myself upright in the sleeping bag as my brain struggled to put the pieces together. Officer Leo didn't dream about a giant anteater. It had been this tapir-like animal that tried to eat my dream.

It was called a baku.

Pops was the one who'd taught me about the supernatural creature that survives by eating dreams. He'd been determined to educate me on every possible monster I might encounter, beginning with the ones most connected to my powers. Although Pops was human, he'd become an expert on the supernatural world. I knew he'd cultivated that particular skill solely for my benefit. Before I was born, he'd been a Navy man, someone who worked with his hands. Academics hadn't been one of his strengths. That all changed when I came along.

I wiggled out of the sleeping bag and searched the house for the baku. I wasn't sure how it entered and exited its victims, whether it had a physical form at all. I checked on Alicia and Renee in the master bedroom. Alicia stirred at the sound of my footsteps, and I took that as a good sign.

I returned downstairs and went outside to walk the perimeter of the house under the watchful eye of the moon. There was no sign of the creature, nor evidence of its recent visit.

The baku had made a fatal error by trying to eat the dreams of the one supernatural in town that could defeat it.

Now I just had to figure out how.

CHAPTER 16

fficer Leo had been the one to mention the anteater dream, which didn't necessarily rule him out as responsible for the current situation. It was possible he'd brought the demon here, or even that he was the demon's human form, although the latter seemed unlikely. I wasn't aware of any records that stated a baku could take human form.

I didn't want to be too obvious about my quest, so I drove Alicia to school and then parked my truck downtown, hoping to see the new cop. Fairhaven was only a town of three thousand people in a contained area. Odds were good that we'd cross paths if I loitered long enough.

I ducked into Five Beans to see whether Officer Leo had picked up Chief Garcia's caffeine habit.

"Lorelei?"

I spun around to see two members of the Assassins Guild. I recognized Alfonso Triton, a tall, solidly built man with black hair and a gold earring, seated at a table with Vaughn, Cam's crush.

"You're not with Cam?" I asked Vaughn as I approached the table.

"I was. Gun's with her now."

"I don't see you out and about very often," Alfonso said. "If you want a hot drink, the chai latte is the ultimate comfort beverage."

"Actually, I was looking for someone, but I don't see him."

He kicked out a chair. "Then sit down and chat with us for a few minutes."

"How's it going?" I said, reluctantly taking a seat between them.

"I heard you stepped up for Dusty," Alfonso said. "That's very cool of you."

"Lorelei is incredibly cool," Vaughn chimed in. "I'm starting to understand why Sullivan has taken an interest."

"I'm sure any of you would've done the same, if you'd been allowed," I said.

"Sullivan would punish the whole guild if one of us broke that particular rule," Alfonso confirmed.

As if on cue, the door to the shop swung open and in walked the prince of hell himself. The sight of this regal demon in the middle of the local coffee shop tickled me and I burst into laughter. The sound of my inelegant cackle drew his attention to our table.

He smiled at the sight of me. "Miss Clay, what a lovely surprise."

"You're late," Vaughn told him.

I narrowed my eyes at the assassins. "You knew he was coming?"

"Did anyone order for me?" Kane asked, joining us.

Alfonso shook his head. "We didn't want yours to get cold. Lorelei hasn't ordered yet either. You can go up to the counter together."

I rose to my feet. "Or I could order for both of us and let the three of you talk."

Kane offered his arm. "Nonsense. I'd be more than happy to escort you."

I ignored his proffered elbow. It was basically a game for him now to see how many ways he could encourage me to make physical contact with him, knowing I'd refuse, although he didn't know why.

"See anything you like?" he asked in a vaguely suggestive tone.

I made a show of staring at the board behind the counter. "If I have to squint to see it, the answer is no."

He laughed. "Fair enough. The mocha with whip is an indulgence I highly recommend."

"Is that what you're getting?"

"No, I'm in the mood for something with cinnamon or nutmeg today."

"Don't tell me you're a pumpkin spice fan."

He shot me a curious look. "What's wrong with that?"

I bit back a smile. "Nothing. Throw on a pair of yoga pants and you're a basic bitch."

Rita motioned for us to step up and order. I opted for the salted caramel latte. I really wanted the mocha but couldn't bring myself to follow Kane's advice on principle.

"A large pumpkin spice latte for me, please," he said.

More like pumpkin spite.

He handed over a twenty-dollar bill before I could even reach for my wallet.

"My treat," he said.

"It seems you're always covering my drinks tab."

"I'm more than equipped to do so."

We moved to the far end of the counter to wait for our drinks, and he pivoted to face me.

"What's so important that you've left your fortress to mix with the population of Fairhaven?" he asked.

"You underestimate the amount of time I spend at home."

"An evasive answer. Interesting." He contemplated me. "You weren't meeting anyone here or you wouldn't have ordered with me."

"Would it bother you if I were?"

"Of course not. What you do is your business, Miss Clay."

"As it happens, I was looking for the new cop, Officer Leo."

"I see. You two have hit it off, have you? Does Magnarella know about your change of heart?"

I rolled my eyes. "Not to date him. To question him about the sleep issue. I guess you've heard about Camryn."

"The guild can talk of little else." The demon frowned. "Why would you question the new recruit? I would think Chief Garcia would be a better source of information."

I decided to share my update with him. It wasn't the kind of information I needed to keep to myself.

"And Officer Leo told you about his anteater dream? That *is* interesting."

"Do you know anything about the baku?"

"Can't say that I do, but if this creature is terrorizing the residents of Fairhaven, I'll have to assert my dominance."

"You're a prince of hell," I reminded him. "That's your territory."

"Except I'm not currently in hell. I'm here."

"For reasons that remain unclear," I added with a pointed look.

"It seems we both have histories we'd like to keep to ourselves," he said.

Our drinks were placed on the counter, and we reached for them simultaneously.

Kane lifted the cup to his lips. "If I didn't know any better, I'd say you were trying to beat me."

"Pretty sure I did. My hand touched the cup first."

"Nonsense. If anything, it was a tie." He advanced toward the table, seemingly in an effort to beat me there too.

I carried my cup past the table as he sat in the chair I had occupied.

"Miss Clay, where are you going?" Kane demanded.

"I need to research the monster."

"It's a giant thingamajig with a funny nose that makes people sleepy. What more do you need to know?"

I cast a look at him over my shoulder. "How to kill it."

I made it halfway to my truck when I spotted Officer Leo issuing a ticket to an illegally parked Audi.

"Hey, Officer Leo," I said, hustling over to him. "Just the guy I wanted to see."

He shook his head. "I swear Audi drivers are the kings of douches. Their entitlement issues make them think they can park wherever they want without consequences." He secured the ticket beneath the windshield wiper.

"I was hoping to talk to you about that dream you had the other night."

He looked momentarily uneasy. "Excuse me?"

"The one about the giant anteater."

Relief passed over his features. "Oh, right. I was worried there for a second."

I didn't want to open that particular can of worms. "Do you recall any details about the anteater? Did it try to suck up things in the dream like a vacuum?"

He scratched the top of his head. "What makes you ask that?"

"Because I had a dream about one, too," I admitted. "I think you must've influenced me."

He offered a crooked smile. "I'm influencing your dreams, huh? Not too many women would admit that."

"It was hardly a pleasant dream, and you weren't in it."

"Too bad." He paused. "Not that I'd want to get sucked up by a giant anteater."

"I think mine was actually more of a tapir, or maybe a baku." I watched his expression closely for any flicker of recognition.

His eyebrows drew together. "I haven't heard of either of those."

"Oh, I was a big animal kingdom fan as a kid. My grandfather taught me about different species from all over the world."

Officer Leo's smile broadened. "I love the zoo. We should go sometime."

"I'm not a fan of zoos. Sorry." The concept of keeping animals in cages for our amusement had always bothered me, even as a child. I think part of me worried that if people found out about me, they'd want to stick me in a cage too.

His face crumpled. "That's cool. I get it." He gestured to the parked cars. "It was great to talk to you, but I need to get moving. These tickets aren't going to write themselves."

I spotted Kane's car a few yards away; the Rolls-Royce Ghost was hard to miss, despite its name. "I think that one might be over the yellow line. You might want to take a look."

"Thanks."

I whistled happily as I headed toward my next destination.

My best bet for information on the baku was the bookshop owned by the oldest human in Fairhaven. Jessie Talbot was enviably sharp for her age. Pops would've liked the old woman. Leather Bound was just around the corner, so I left my truck in its spot, making sure it was nice and legally parked first, and walked to the bookshop with my latte.

Jessie clapped her hands as I entered. "Roll out the red carpet. The queen of the castle has arrived."

"I'm never going to live that down, am I?"

"You're a single young woman who bought Bluebeard's Castle," Jessie said. "What did you expect?"

A thought occurred to me. "Did you know the original owners?"

"Joseph Edgar Blue III was before my time, but I remember the stories about him trotting out his medium to contact the spirits and entertain his guests."

"You don't believe it was real?"

"Not with that fraudulent huckster he hired. History reveals all, my dear. It doesn't mean I don't believe in psychic phenomenon, of course. Living here, you can't help but notice strange occurrences."

Instead of moving straight to the stacks, I found myself inching closer to the chair where she sat beside the counter. A cane rested against the wall next to her.

"You've mentioned that before," I said.

"I'm not surprised. You name it and someone in Fairhaven has experienced it."

"Have you had any experiences with strange dreams or even lack of dreams lately?"

She offered a wistful smile. "My dreams are always of the past. Parties and paramours. The vivid ones are my favorite. It's like my lost loved ones are with me again."

I knew what she meant. A few specific piano chords and my grandmother was right beside me again.

"I take it you're not here to learn about my personal history, as scintillating as it is." She waved a hand. "If you find a book you want and there's no price, just ask me."

"You mean it isn't free?" I joked.

She laughed. "You'd like that, wouldn't you? The upkeep alone on your house must cost a small fortune."

"I have money set aside for the expenses, although it seems to be running out faster than I expected."

Jessie laughed again. "Money has a way of doing that. What are you searching for today? Maybe I can point you in the right direction."

"Information on a creature called a baku."

"Don't think I'm familiar with that one. Do you know the country of origin? Baku, you said? Sounds Japanese."

"It is. Very good."

"Don't give me too much credit. One of my great-grand-children likes to draw in that anime style, and I think she may have told me one of the weird creatures she drew was called a baku."

I froze. "Was this recent?"

"Why do you think I remember? It was yesterday. My grandson brought Kelsey here while he went to a job interview. She wasn't feeling well, so he didn't send her to school." Jessie shook her head. "In my day, we could have snot running out of every pore of our body and we still went to school."

I smiled. "Is that the medical equivalent of walking uphill in snow both ways?"

"Pretty much."

"Did Kelsey happen to leave the drawings behind?"

Jessie perked up. "As a matter of fact, she left one of them stuck to the mini fridge in the back room." She reached for her cane, but I stopped her.

"I can get it, if you don't mind me going back there."

"Have at it. I've got nothing to hide back there except my dentures case."

I skirted the counter and walked through the open doorway that led to the employee-only space. The fridge was so small that the sheet of paper nearly blocked my view of it.

Kelsey was a talented artist. The baku looked exactly like the one in my dream. The drawing showed the creature standing face-to-face with a unicorn in front of a rainbow.

I returned to Jessie with the drawing in hand. "This is very good. How old is Kelsey?"

"Ten."

"Did she seem well when she was here, or do you think she just wanted to get out of school?"

"She seemed more tired than usual. Other than that, I think she was fine. I imagine she was up late the night before and was paying the price for it. Her parents aren't the best when it comes to a strict schedule. I told them she couldn't come back today if she decides to stay home again because

I'm going to visit my friend Harriet." The wrinkles of Jessie's pruned face tightened. "Harriet slipped into a coma the other night. She'd been unwell, but we didn't realize how bad it was until then."

"I'm sorry to hear that," I said. "Does she live in Fairhaven?"

"Yes, she's in one of the townhouses. She has a home health aide coming to check on her, and her son and daughter-in-law have moved in temporarily. They were going to take her to a hospital, but she has a living will that limits her treatment. If she doesn't wake up soon, that's it for poor Harriet." Jessie sounded vaguely fatigued by the notion, like she'd attended more than her share of funerals.

"I hope she wakes up soon then."

Worry gnawed at me as the pressure began to build. I had to find a way to rouse these women from their unintended slumbers. I also didn't want young Kelsey or anyone else to suffer the same fate as Renee, Cam, and Harriet. The only way to protect them was to find the baku and kill it before it caused any further damage to people. I wasn't sure how many baku visits it took to trigger a coma, nor did I know how many Kelsey had already experienced.

"Now that I think about it, I've got a small Japanese mythology section." Jessie pointed to my left. "One stack over. Far right. Middle shelf."

"Do you have this whole place memorized?"

Her thin lips stretched into a smile. "Only the books that haven't been moved in twenty years."

I followed her instructions and located the section easily. I dusted off the fattest book I could find and flipped to the index. Bingo.

I skimmed the contents of the page. Some of the information was as I remembered—the baku devours dreams and nightmares. According to Japanese legend, the supernatural beings were created by the gods using the leftover pieces of other animals. Those gods must've had a lot of leftover tapir and anteater pieces, although this book suggested a baku consisted of an elephant's trunk, an ox's tail, and tiger paws. The book had to have been written by humans who'd never actually seen one. It happened a lot. I only hoped the rest of their information was accurate because I was relying on it to save lives.

The more I read, the more confused I was. A baku should only come when summoned, traditionally by children for protection against nightmares. They'd place a talisman by their bedside to call to a baku for help. The only warning was not to become overly reliant on the creature because it might eat more than the nightmare if it was still hungry afterward.

For whatever reason, the Fairhaven baku was on a bender.

I closed the book and replaced it on the shelf. Killing the baku appeared to be the only way to defeat it, which seemed a shame. There had to be a good reason this baku was eating its way through the residents of Fairhaven to the point where some of them had become comatose, and I began to worry I knew what that good reason was. If the baku was used as protection from nightmares, then it was also meant to protect people from me. What if neither Officer Leo nor Naomi Smith were to blame for the baku's presence?

What if the responsible party was me?

CHAPTER 17

I set my concerns aside and focused on rooting out the baku to defeat it before it harmed anyone else. I left the bookshop and drove straight home to think. Seated at my kitchen table, I updated West on the new information without mentioning my presence as the potential trigger. West had already made it clear he didn't want me here if my presence endangered the town. If he knew about my connection to the baku, the alpha wouldn't hesitate to run me out of Fairhaven.

"Sounds like you've had a breakthrough," Ray said, appearing by the fridge.

I nodded. "I need a talisman to summon the baku."

"What kind of talisman?" Ray asked.

"It's specific to a baku. Japanese children would put it next to their beds to summon the creature and have it devour their bad dreams."

"It seems to be eating what it wants without the talisman," Ray said. "What good will it do now?"

"It'll summon the baku to the place I want it."

His eyebrows crept up to his hairline. "I see. And then you'll kill it?" He hesitated. "How do you kill something that isn't real?"

"Oh, it's real. It just exists in another plane. That's how it gets inside everyone's heads without breaking into their houses first."

"And you can kill this thing in a dream state?" Ray looked dubious of my claim.

"If it doesn't devour me first."

"Why would it do that? It doesn't seem to be devouring anybody else, unless you mean you might end up in a coma."

I didn't mean that, but I didn't want to worry Ray any more than I already had. "We're going to summon the baku so I can kill it, and then Renee will wake up." Along with the others who'd been affected. I hoped.

He nodded. "I believe you, Lorelei."

I was glad somebody did, because I was having serious doubts I could pull this off. I was the baku's natural nemesis. Now that I knew that, I was surprised it ran away from me in my dream. My unexpected appearance must've caught it off guard. I wouldn't get that grace period twice.

"Know where you can get the talisman?" Ray asked.

"Not yet, but I have a few ideas." I swiped my keys off the counter and strode toward the door.

"I wish I could come with you."

If I commanded it, he could, but I didn't want him to know that. Some secrets had to be kept for the greater good, and that was one of them.

"You're better off here with your daughter," I said. "I'll be back as soon as I can."

I rode my motorcycle to the Devil's Playground. It was faster, and I wanted this visit to be quick and painless. I hated to involve the demon in any way, but he was in the best position to locate a talisman quickly.

Josie was by the door when I arrived.

"Hey, Josie."

The vampire barely acknowledged me as I breezed past her.

Kane wasn't behind the bar as I expected. Instead, he sat on the bench at the piano. Hope flared that he would put his fingers to the keys and produce a horrible sound that would make him forever unattractive to me.

Naturally, he was amazing.

Bastard.

He stopped playing. "You've brought news about the party responsible for Camryn's condition, I assume."

"I've identified the creature."

"That's all? I assume you would've learned how to kill the beast before you raced over here."

"I did my research," I said.

"And?" he prompted.

"I need your help."

He stared at me for an extra beat. "Is that new for you? Evidence of personal growth?" He didn't wait for an answer. "Any requests? If I recall correctly, you have a fondness for classical music. Debussy, was it?"

"You remember that?" I'd once mentioned to Kane that Debussy reminded me of my grandmother.

He responded by playing the beginning of *Clair de Lune*.

"Not that one," I said quickly.

His fingers deftly changed course and he switched to *Reverie* without a moment's hesitation. "Better?" he asked.

"Yes." The piece stirred my emotions, albeit less painfully than *Clair de Lune*. Where *Clair de Lune* brought me to my knees, *Reverie* raised me to my feet.

"One of these days, we'll have to chat more about music, when there isn't a creature to slay." His fingers dropped to rest on his lap.

Part of me longed for him to keep playing, but I knew it would be a mistake. I told him about the baku and my need for a talisman.

"And you believe this would help wake Camryn?"

"And the others."

He observed me. "Well done, Miss Clay."

"Not so fast. I haven't defeated it yet."

"Maybe not, but you've given us more of a lead than anyone's developed so far. A baku never would've occurred to me."

"Can you find a talisman?" If anybody had the kind of connections necessary to locate a talisman at a moment's notice, it was the prince of hell.

Kane regarded me. "The baku has already visited you. Another encounter could leave you in a coma."

"I'm aware of that."

Josie joined us at the piano. "Tell me where it is, and I'll bring it for you."

The vampire was as desperate to get rid of me as West. She had good instincts; I'd give her that. No wonder she was Kane's head of security.

"Allow me to use the talisman. I'm a prince of hell. The baku doesn't stand a chance."

"As tempting as your offer is, I'm the one who needs to handle it."

"Why you? You didn't bring it here." His gaze intensified. "Or did you? Not deliberately, of course. Did you accidentally summon it somehow?"

I couldn't tell him the truth. "I think I might have."

"You shouldn't put yourself in harm's way because of guilt, not when someone else is equally capable of doing the job."

"This is my mess. I need to clean it up." Now that I knew more about the baku, I felt convinced its arrival was no coincidence. The baku was here because of me.

Kane heaved a sigh in frustration. "If you won't let me do it, then at least talk to West. It sounds like his wolves have been affected as well."

"I thought you two hated each other." As the alpha of the

local Arrowhead werewolf pack, Weston Davies wasn't a big fan of the prince of hell.

"I don't hate anybody," Kane said. "Hate is wasted energy."

"He hates you," Josie said, pressing down on a piano key. I got the sense she enjoyed telling her boss that someone disliked him.

"West will do what's necessary for the safety of his pack," Kane said, ignoring Josie.

"I don't need West. I said I'd do it, and that's final."

Josie snorted. "It was nice knowing you, Clay. Just out of curiosity, who gets your house if you die?"

"Miss Clay doesn't require a Last Will and Testament, Josephine. She'll be fine."

"My lawyer says everybody needs one." She cocked her head at Kane. "Do you have one? Who gets the club if you die?"

Kane laughed shortly. "If I die? Listen to yourself."

"What if you become incapacitated like Cam?"

"Dantalion will take my place, should that day ever come, which it won't."

Josie whistled. "You'd let Danny Boy run the club? That's brave."

"Then who would take his place in hell?" I asked. "Doesn't he lord over all those legions of demons?" I'd met Dantalion a couple months ago, and the great duke of hell was only too happy to tell me about his weighty responsibilities.

"Those details do not require your attention," Kane said in a tone that suggested the conversation was over. "Suffice it to say, Dantalion quite enjoys his current position."

"That's Kane for you," Josie said with a rare smile. "He can make death and dismemberment seem like a casual picnic by the lake."

Kane rose from the bench. "Permit me to make a few calls."

I waited by the piano as he paced the club floor, making one call after another. After about fifteen minutes of Josie snarling at me, he returned to the piano. "If you'll join me at the crossroads, I've sourced this talisman for you."

I nodded. "Thanks, Kane. I appreciate your willingness to get involved."

"And I appreciate that you can bring yourself to acknowledge it instead of pretending it didn't happen," he replied.

"That feels like a backhanded compliment."

"You two are exhausting," Josie complained.

"Hold down the fort, Josephine," Kane advised. "Once again, Miss Clay and I are on a mission to save the residents of Fairhaven. It's becoming quite a habit, isn't it?"

I didn't respond.

I left my motorcycle at the club, and we walked through the woods to the crossroads.

"Ah, here he is now," Kane said.

A cloaked figure emerged from between the trees. Wordlessly, bony fingers stretched to place an item in Kane's open hand. Wordlessly, the figure passed back through the crossroads.

Kane held up the talisman. "I believe this is what you need."

I stared at the small carving of the monstrous beast. It was the warped version of the baku as described in Jessie's mythology book. I didn't think it mattered, though.

"What's next?" Kane asked.

I plucked the talisman from his hand. "Just watch over me and make sure I don't die."

He smirked. "Am I allowed to perform mouth-to-mouth should things take a turn?"

I held up a finger. "If and only if I'm on the verge of death."

"Noted."

I sat and leaned against the base of a large oak tree.

"Is that comfortable, Miss Clay?"

I looked at him. "I'm summoning a baku, not enjoying a spa day."

I closed my eyes and focused on the talisman. I wasn't sure how long it took me to fall asleep; either way, the baku was a no-show. I walked through my dreams, visiting more than one during my search for the creature. The baku apparently refused to be summoned.

I opened my eyes to see Kane's whisky-colored eyes staring down at me with a concerned expression.

"No baku?" he asked.

"No baku." It was odd. The talisman should have worked, unless the baku somehow knew I was on the hunt.

My phone buzzed, momentarily distracting me from my failure. My heart lodged in my throat when I saw Albert's name on the screen.

"You look like you've seen a ghost you weren't expecting, Miss Clay. What is it?"

It was showtime, but I couldn't tell him that. I scrambled to my feet. "I need to go."

"What about the baku?"

I stuffed the talisman in my pocket. "I'll try again later."

"Not without supervision. It's too dangerous," he said.

And so was the next opponent I was about to face.

CHAPTER 18

managed to dodge all Kane's questions as we left the crossroads. I was relieved when I finally arrived at my motorcycle and could escape his inquisition.

I rode as fast as I could to reach the Castle before Albert did. By the time I entered the house, I had a message from Gun to say that he and Dusty were about to be escorted to the private location.

I barely had time to shove a handful of blueberries in my mouth and down a glass of water when I received a text that Albert had arrived. I shook off my nerves and strode to the sedan outside the gate.

Albert offered an encouraging smile. "How are you feeling, champ?"

"Like I'm being arrested and will need to fight my way out of prison."

His head bobbed. "I can see that."

I slid into the passenger seat and closed the door. "Do you need to blindfold me?"

"No." He pressed a button, and all the windows became too tinted to see through, including the driver's portion.

"Um… This seems problematic," I said.

He settled against the seat. "It's like driving on autopilot. The car goes where it needs to go, and nobody's the wiser." He glanced at me. "It's perfectly safe. Mr. Magnarella isn't going to risk injuring his moneymaker."

I double-checked my seatbelt and tried to relax.

"It isn't too far." He reached into a duffel bag and produced a snack. "Glazed donut?"

"No, thank you."

He took a generous bite. "I'm rooting for you, Lorelei," he said, although it was hard to understand him with all the donut in his mouth.

The car finally came to a stop, and Albert walked around to open my door. I was amazed to see we were either inside a building or underground. There were no distinguishing features to note.

"This way," Albert urged.

I followed him through a doorway to where Dr. Edmonds and Imani awaited me.

He broke into a pleased grin. "There she is. Our future champion."

"I bet you say that to all the girls."

"He does," Imani said, unsmiling.

"Albert, please wait outside to escort Miss Clay to the ring."

Imani handed me a square of folded red material. "You need to change into this. Leave your shoes. You both fight barefoot."

"Your opponent will be wearing a green version of the same outfit," Dr. Edmonds added.

Imani motioned to the screen divider. "Behind there. Hurry."

I darted behind the screen and changed into the top and matching shorts. The material was soft like cotton, but I sensed a magical quality to it that I assumed allowed for shifting. I didn't want to risk losing the talisman, so I took it from the pocket of my sweatpants and shoved it into the shorts. It produced a slight bulge that made my hip appear slightly lumpy.

I emerged from behind the screen, and Dr. Edmonds held out a cup that measured about thirty milliliters of clear liquid. "Your elixir, Miss Clay."

I sniffed the contents. "Candy cane. I'm not going to turn into Santa Claus, am I?"

"I believe the scent you mean is peppermint," Imani said without humor.

"This isn't Freyja?"

"Not this time. Drink up," Dr. Edmonds urged. "It's almost time and you want the elixir through your system when it starts."

I really didn't.

I drank the elixir under his watchful eye and handed him the empty cup. Imani opened the door.

"Make us proud," Dr. Edmonds said.

It took every ounce of strength not to kick him in the teeth.

Albert patted my back as I started down the corridor. "The crowd will seem intimidating at first, but you'll get used to it pretty quickly."

"How long will the match last?"

"Depends. I've seen a couple go for hours, but most are finished in under sixty minutes." He guided me to a small area outside a large set of steel doors. "Consider this the green room."

"I thought my opponent was green."

Albert frowned. "No, I mean like in television. Never mind." He glanced over his shoulder. "I'm going to check that we're running on schedule. I'll be right back."

I paced the floor, trying to keep my wits about me. I'd suppress the new powers with the same level of control I'd adopted for my own. I had no intention of using them. I could go down early and let my opponent win before either one of us got too banged up. There was nothing about the arrangement that stipulated I had to win, only to compete.

A knock on the wall startled me. My eyes nearly bugged out of my head when I saw Kane standing there. "You've got to be kidding me. What in the prince of hell are you doing here?"

"Funny. That was my question for you."

I looked past him for any sign of Albert. "You can't be here, Kane."

He held up a golden ticket. "It seems I can."

I snatched the ticket from his hand. "Where did you get this?"

I bought it off the demon on her way inside the building. "Very pricey affair you're hosting."

I laughed. "You think I'm hosting this?"

He plucked the ticket from my fingers and tucked it safely in his pocket. "I'd like an explanation."

"I don't owe you one."

"No, but I'm asking anyway."

"Because you're a prince and you demand obedience?"

His gaze softened. "Because I thought you and I... I thought you were my friend."

Okay, that got me. "I'm not a host. I'm a participant. And you shouldn't have followed me."

"You shouldn't have acted so cagey when you received the phone call at the crossroads. A participant in what?"

"Some kind of deity fight. I drank an elixir that will give me the power of a god, and then I fight someone else who does the same thing. Bets are placed. Somebody wins. Show over."

His brow creased. "I don't like the sound of this already. Is this why you met with Magnarella? Why would you agree to participate in a farce like this?"

"Because if I don't, someone else would've suffered the consequences."

The muscle in his cheek twitched. "This is it. This is the secret you've been hiding."

I bit my tongue. I made it this far; I wasn't throwing Gunther and Dusty under the bus now.

"Lorelei, finally. I've been looking everywhere for you. You should see the crowd out there. It's insane." Gunther slid to a stop behind Kane. "Oh, boy. I didn't expect to see you here."

"Me neither," I said pointedly.

A white swan waddled next to Gunther. "I sure hope you win because I'm sick and tired of honking when I want to curse instead."

Turning to face them, Kane folded his arms. "I'm beginning to get the picture."

The swan looked up at Kane. "Uh-oh."

"Dusty Saxon, isn't it?"

"Honk, honk," she said feebly.

Gunther shot a panicked look at his sister. "I can explain," he said.

"No need. Let me see if I understand the situation." Kane pointed at the swan. "You tried to steal an item of value from Vincenzo Magnarella and somehow found yourself turned into a swan. You were doomed to stay a swan unless someone took your place in this ungodly fight. Enter Lorelei Clay."

Gunther winced. "In a nutshell." I was relieved that he didn't mention payment. The fact that I was accepting money for this made me feel even worse.

Kane glanced at me. "When did you become friends with Dusty?"

I sighed. "When she showed up at my house as a swan."

Kane pressed his lips together. I couldn't tell whether he was suppressing a laugh or abject disappointment. "How did she ring the bell? With her beak?"

"I carried her," Gun admitted.

He gripped the edge of the wall. "You carried…" He shut

up and pinched the bridge of his nose to regain his composure. "Gunther, I don't even know where to begin."

"He didn't do anything wrong," I intervened. "He came to me for help out of respect for your gentleman's agreement."

Kane eyed the assassin. "Why did you rope in Miss Clay?"

"Because nobody else would agree to help."

Kane pivoted to me. "And why did you? Aren't you supposed to be locked away in your tower, avoiding humanity?"

"He appealed to my bank account," I admitted.

"I see." Kane took a menacing step toward Gun. "The next time you find yourself between a rock and a hard place, you come to me."

"But the rules…"

"I am aware of the rules because I set them. I am also the head of the guild."

"This isn't guild business," I said. "Dusty isn't a member."

"Maybe not, but the guild is the reason why you are about to enter into some ridiculously dangerous and unnecessary competition that could kill you. Therefore, it is guild business."

"I'm sorry, Kane," Gunther said. "I had to help my sister. I didn't want her to get in trouble."

"Or you," Kane added sharply. "Let's not forget that you didn't want to get in trouble either, which is why you went behind my back. Never do it again. And whatever you agreed to pay Miss Clay, I order you to double it."

"This is all my fault," Dusty said. "I knew Magnarella's reputation, but I thought I was smart enough to outwit him."

"Take your feathered friend and go," Kane advised. "I'd like a word with Miss Clay before she puts herself in harm's way."

The swan jumped into Gun's arms, and he whisked her away, leaving me alone with the enraged demon.

"Don't be angry with them. If you want to be mad at someone, I'm the one who lied to you."

The demon snarled. "Don't you dare tell me how to handle my affairs. Gunther Saxon is an assassin under my care. I will deal with the situation as I see fit."

His temper pissed me off. Here I was about to step into a dog fight where I could end up as a divine Rottweiler or a poodle, and Kane was worried about his precious ego. "Maybe if you handled situations better, Gun wouldn't have felt the need to go behind your back."

His nostrils flared with indignation. She shoots and she scores.

"It's one thing to keep secrets," he said. "It's quite another to lie."

"I lied to protect them from your wrath, and judging from what I just saw, I was right to do it."

He drew closer. "Miss Clay. Lorelei, please. You don't understand."

"Heavy is the head that wears the crown. Is that it? Believe me, Kane. I understand more than you know."

His whisky-colored eyes threatened to burn a hole straight through my heart. "You're still going to compete."

"I have no choice. This is Dusty's ticket to freedom. I won't screw it up for her." Even though I might screw up my own in the process.

"I'll speak to Magnarella."

"It's too late. I drank the elixir. There's no way he'll agree to stop the fight now. There's too much money at stake for him." Not to mention the repercussions of interfering could be a higher price than Kane was prepared to pay.

The demon moved his hands to cup my face, prompting me to step backward out of reach.

"You can't kiss me, Kane."

He attempted a wry smile. "Your lips look chapped. I thought I'd moisten them for you."

"I appreciate the good luck gesture…"

"It isn't for luck." He paused. "It isn't *only* for luck. Have I gotten our signals crossed? Because I was beginning to feel confident you were right there with me."

As much as I hated to admit it, I was. Every step of the frustrating way.

"I'm sorry," I said. "It just isn't possible."

"I assure you it is. I can demonstrate if necessary."

Somewhere in the distance, a bell clanged. "The fight's about to start."

"Clay, you're up!" A voice jolted me out of my own head. Albert looked startled to see Kane. "How did you get back here?"

"He got lost trying to find his seat," I said.

"Hurry up and go through the door at the end of the hall. If anyone else sees you, they'll toss you out, and you might not make it with all your limbs intact."

Kane kept his gaze on me. "I'll take my chances."

"Come on, Clay. Show 'em what you're made of." Albert steered me to the doorway. I didn't have the stomach to look back.

I hurt his ego, nothing more.

Kane Sullivan wasn't accustomed to rejection. That was my whole appeal. A powerful woman who didn't fall at his feet. The second I jumped into his arms, I would lose my shine like all the women who came before me. Of course, that wasn't the reason I had to say no. If he knew the truth, he'd understand.

At least I hoped he would.

I followed the noise of the crowd until the heavy metal doors creaked open. Albert nudged me forward into a set of glaring lights.

Showtime.

Cheers erupted as I made my way to the ring. My opponent was already there—a muscular blonde with a scar down her cheek in the shape of a lightning bolt. Her impressive physique gave me pause.

Albert moved to stand in front of me, cutting off my view. "How do you feel?" he asked.

"Like I have no clue what's going on. Why is she so ripped?" I gestured toward my opponent.

"Don't worry about Kaleigh. You're strong, Clay. I've seen your stats."

They only knew a fraction of what I was capable of, and I had to keep it that way.

"Wait. That's Kaleigh?" I peered around him. "That's the one you mentioned during my assessment."

"Really? What did I say?"

"That her stats were excellent." And now I could see why. I thought Dr. Edmond's comment about not being a betting man had been an offhand remark, not an actual reflection of the event. I should've known better.

Albert gripped my arms and tried to hold my attention. "When the bell rings again, you go out there and fight until it's over. The enclosure is warded so the fight stays contained and so do you."

"What qualifies as over?"

His face hardened. "When one of you goes down and doesn't get up again."

I stared back at him. "This isn't MMA-style. This is a death match."

"Not any death match. This is where we lesser beings get to witness the fury of the gods as they battle for dominance."

"Why bother with elixirs? Why not have us fight the old-fashioned way?"

"Because anybody can host a match like that. Do you have any idea how much money spectators are willing to pay to see a divine brawl?"

"But it isn't really. Kaleigh isn't a god. You're sacrificing innocent lives as entertainment."

He arched an eyebrow. "Innocent? No one who steps inside the ring is innocent. That's how you end up here in the first place."

"Oh, so they make a mistake or a bad decision and, naturally, they deserve to die? Is that your take?"

"Do you think they allowed you to participate without finding out more about you first?"

"And what did you discover about me that was so bad that I deserve to be killed for your entertainment?"

"Nothing specific, but I know you don't burn through multiple schools and foster homes if you're a model kid."

His answer took my breath away. "You have no idea why I changed schools so many times. For the record, it wasn't a disciplinary issue."

"Doesn't matter now. Get in there and fulfill your obligation. I believe in you."

It took all my self-control not to break his nose. Shame on me for falling for his friendly act. History had taught me better than that.

"To the victor go the spoils," he said with a half-hearted salute.

I pushed past Albert and walked to the entrance marked with red.

Gunther appeared beside me. "Everything okay? You look pissed as hell."

"Do you understand what's about to happen?" I asked quietly.

"There's a fight. One of you wins. Money exchanges hands. My sister lives. You get paid. Does that cover the salient points?"

"Not quite."

He leaned closer. "What is it?"

"Stay with Dusty. If this goes tits up at any point, I want you to take her and run. Don't wait for me."

"But what about Magnarella?"

"He's not your problem."

"He will be if you break our deal."

I fixed him with my most earnest expression. "Listen to me, Gun. I'll make sure I fulfill the contract for Dusty's sake, but there's a chance things are going to get ugly in here. I don't want you two to get hurt."

"Then let me help. This face can't do ugly, but I have other abilities."

I patted his cheek. "I know you do, and I want you to use them to save your sister."

He withdrew. "Break a leg, Lorelei. Preferably your opponent's."

I turned to face the ring. My mind was a blur of ideas. Unfortunately, not one of them ended with Kaleigh and I leaving the ring unscathed.

My gut twisted when I spotted Naomi Smith in the stands. What was the investigator for The Corporation doing here? I gave her what she wanted. Why hadn't she left town?

This was bad news.

Very bad.

It was too late to turn back now. I had to follow through with the plan and hope for the best. If everything went smoothly, Smith would believe the same as everybody else, that the elixir was the source of my powers.

The second bell rang. The crowd broke into hoots and applause. I entered the ring and felt the crackle of magic as the ward closed around me.

My opponent and I took a moment to scrutinize each other. The condescending curl of her lip told me she liked her odds. I was back in high school, getting sized up by the members of the cool girls' table. It didn't faze me then and it sure as shit didn't faze me now.

I don't want to hurt you.

Albert whistled and Kaleigh's demeanor changed. She paced the edge of the cage like a stressed animal that had disconnected from her surroundings. The hair on the back of my neck responded to the seemingly innocuous repetition. I was trapped in an enclosure with a stressed-out deity.

No good could come from this.

The sooner I knew which god I was fighting, the sooner I knew whether her sneer was justified.

Her mouth split open, releasing a breath as hot as a desert wind. There was only one goddess I associated with that particular talent.

Sekhmet.

Kaleigh had the power of the Egyptian goddess of war and disease, a goddess that nearly destroyed all of humanity.

Terrific.

I knew what Sekhmet was capable of. The more important question was—did Kaleigh? My best hope was that she wasn't as knowledgeable about her abilities as I was and wouldn't tap into the more potent ones.

The warded enclosure prevented the scorching air from harming the spectators. Too bad. I would've liked to see them scatter. I was horrified by anyone who considered this a form of entertainment. It would be different if Magnarella chose volunteers, but instead he took advantage of women in vulnerable situations. I'd like to see him become the chew toy of the gods.

I glanced in the stands to see the swan seated beside Gunther. Dusty wouldn't have survived this.

"Do something!" a voice yelled. Male, of course.

Kaleigh responded to the demand by morphing into an enormous lioness with a golden coat. Lioness powers—check.

I danced backward as far as the enclosure allowed. I didn't want to harm Kaleigh; it wasn't her fault she'd been pitted against me. By the same token, if I didn't defend myself, she'd kill me.

The lioness lunged. I jumped to the side, hoping Kaleigh would slam into the ward and knock herself out.

No such luck.

The lioness was agile enough to turn before she hit the ward. Her body whirled toward me with unexpected speed. Her mouth gaped open and released a deafening roar.

I crouched low to the mat, debating my options. Sadly, that thought experiment didn't take long.

The lioness stalked toward me. The size of one paw was larger than my head. One good swat with those claws and it was goodbye noggin.

I sprang first and launched myself onto her back. The crowd went wild.

"Didn't expect that, did you?" I dug my heels sharply into her sides.

The lioness twisted and snapped her jaws. I'd ridden my share of bucking broncos; Pops had insisted on it. He may not have anticipated this particular scenario, but he certainly seemed to know the types of challenges I'd one day face.

The lioness dropped to her side and started to roll, pinning my foot between her body and the mat. I ignored the painful snap and managed to dislodge my foot.

I dragged myself across the mat, vaguely aware of voices outside the ward calling for my god to come out and play. I resisted.

The lioness's mouth opened again. This time, instead of a roar, I heard Kaleigh's voice, low and urgent. "I know what you're trying to do, and it won't work. Only one of us is leaving here. I don't care if you refuse to fight. I'm not willing to die today."

No one else could've heard her over the din of the crowd. "I don't want either one of us to die today, Kaleigh."

Her eyes flashed with anger. "If I have to do this, then at least don't make me feel bad about it." She raised her head and roared with a ferocity that shook the enclosure. The spectators hooted and stomped their feet in return.

"Fight me or die!" she rasped. The lioness charged.

I remained firmly planted and ignored the throbbing of my foot.

Closer.

Closer.

Curling my fingers together, I stepped aside at the last second and used my hands as a club, slamming them down on the lioness's spine as she passed. The lioness fell to the mat, immobile.

Applause shook the enclosure.

I shot a quick glance at Albert. Kaleigh was down and not getting up. Maybe they would agree to end the match without the need for death.

Cheers erupted again. At first, I thought they were for me until I turned to watch the lioness transform back into Kaleigh as she pulled herself to her feet. It seemed the match wasn't over after all.

Her body swayed from the effort. Pain was etched in her features. I wasn't sure what she intended to do until her skin began to glow with a golden light.

Every muscle in my body tightened.

Sekhmet had the ability to produce the power of the midday sun, and it seemed Kaleigh had decided to go nuclear. The goddess's body might be able to survive such a transformation, but the supernatural's body couldn't, no matter how impressive her stats.

A hush fell over the crowd.

"Kaleigh, don't!" I pleaded.

Her eyes burned ruby red. She was too far gone to heed my advice. The elixir had corrupted her ability to think rationally.

A blast of heat rushed toward me, and I dropped to the mat to avoid it. If I didn't handle this right, Kaleigh was going to kill us both.

The spectators started to chant Sekhmet's name. They were lucky the real goddess wasn't here. She'd smite them all in a single breath. Supernaturals and humans had no idea what they'd be up against if the deities ever returned to reclaim the world they lost.

I braced myself as light blasted from the would-be goddess, blinding me. I felt my body lift off the ground. The world fell silent. I wasn't sure when I landed, or whether I was still airborne. Pain radiated through me, so much of it that the injuries blended together into one giant thrum.

Sekhmet for the win.

Through the void, I heard the familiar dreamlike sound of *Reverie*. It seemed that Death had come to escort me home.

The piano chords poked me gently. A vision of my grandmother flashed in my mind. "You must practice, Lorelei," she said. "It's the only way to improve."

I smelled the stench of charred skin. Felt a rubbery surface against my skin.

The music wasn't accompanying me to the Great Beyond; it was keeping me anchored to the earth, to this plane.

Slowly, I opened my eyes to locate the source of the sound. The spectators were a blur, save one. No one seemed to notice the well-dressed demon with the phone in his hand. My eyes locked on Kane's. He didn't smile or yell my name.

I clawed the mat and pulled myself to an upright position. The crowd lost their minds. Kaleigh wailed her displeasure.

Without touching me, Kane had raised me to my feet.

My emotions rushed to the surface, too powerful to stop. This was the reason I avoided music, especially now when I was too weak to keep my walls intact. All at once, they came crashing down. I let the music move through me until it penetrated my soul and coaxed me back to life.

Then I turned up the dial.

My body blurred as I sped toward my opponent. I threw myself on top of Kaleigh and spread my fingers across her face. I slipped into her head with ease. The interior was a jumble of images, presumably because of the elixir, but I located Kaleigh's nightmare and ripped open the fabric between dreams and reality.

I didn't miss Albert's stunned expression just outside the ward. There was only one goddess with this ability, and it was highly unlikely they'd crafted an elixir for her.

Because I was standing right here.

I moved to the side and observed the army of large, hairy spiders as they crawled over their target. I was in no danger; they would respond to my commands if necessary.

But it wasn't necessary.

It was painful to watch Kaleigh succumb to her worst fear. Anguished screams tore from her throat as she huddled in the corner in the fetal position. I hoped she knew I took no pleasure in this. At least the spiders weren't venomous. Worst case scenario was that Kaleigh would pass out and the match would be forced to end.

The ward around us sizzled and sparked. I looked down at my bare feet just as the mat below me sent an electric current up my spine—and everything went black.

CHAPTER 19

My eyelids fluttered open. I expected to see a stadium of spectators peering down at me with anticipation, except I was no longer in the ring. I was strapped to a table in the lab at the compound.

Dr. Edmonds turned to smile at me from his position at the monitor. "Welcome back, Clay."

I wiggled my fingers. "I'm not dead."

"An incredible match. Unprecedented, in fact."

Across the room, I spotted Kaleigh strapped to a table. "Is she alive?"

"Oh, yes. We stopped the match when we realized she was paralyzed by fear." He glanced at me. "Very clever, by the way, especially since the elixir you drank provided no such ability."

I didn't respond.

"How did you do it?"

I ignored the question. "The match is over. We fulfilled our contracts. Let us go."

"I'm afraid there's been a change in plans." He prepared a syringe. "Consider yourself fortunate. You're about to witness the true purpose of the match, a higher calling than mere financial gain."

"I'd rather meditate, thanks."

"You'll get your wish soon enough."

I squinted at him. "What's that supposed to mean?"

He walked toward Kaleigh with the syringe. "It means my experiments serve a greater purpose than simply lining Mr. Magnarella's silk pockets."

"Yeah, I got that part. What's the greater purpose?"

"A new world order, given time."

I groaned. "Because that always goes well."

He craned his neck to look at me. "You're mouthy for someone strapped to a table."

"Blame my grandfather. He wasn't big on manners. What's in the syringe?"

"Step one of Kaleigh's ascension. A new elixir I've been developing alongside the one you took."

I didn't like the sound of that. I glanced at Kaleigh. "How is this new one different from the one you already gave her?"

He hovered beside an unconscious Kaleigh with the syringe in hand. "I'm so glad you asked. This one does far more than replicate a godly power or two. It is, in fact, the very essence of the deity. Kaleigh will act as a host to the actual goddess, one who is no longer capable of returning to this realm in her original form."

"I'll pass on that plan. I'm not really in the market for a roommate." I tilted my head. "No vacancy at the inn."

"Which is why I've developed this very complex procedure. Kaleigh's consciousness will move to the back, creating a vacuum for the goddess to fill. The lucky deity is then given a new lease on her immortal life." He leered at me. "Would you like to know which goddess won the auction for Kaleigh's body? I don't usually offer such information, but it was quite a competition this time. You both impressed them. Mr. Magnarella was irate when neither of you died, until I told him about the results of the auction. That seemed to placate him."

"Lucky us. We're the prize pigs at the fair."

"Alakshmi has chosen to inhabit Kaleigh."

The name would've paralyzed me, if I hadn't already been strapped to a table.

"Do you know who she is?"

"Goddess of misery, poverty, and grief? Leaves a trail of jealousy and malice in her wake wherever she goes? That Alakshmi?"

His face reflected surprise. "Your knowledge of deities is impressive, Clay. I don't normally meet women in your position with that level of knowledge."

"I know a lot of things, like the fact you're a world class douchecanoe."

"How did you manage to display that unexpected ability? Was it magic?"

I jerked my head to the side to avoid eye contact.

"You may as well tell me the truth. No one is coming to save you."

"You're right. Because I'm what people need saving from."

He laughed at that. "Save the attitude, Clay. The elixir was designed to wear off by now, and those straps are stronger than Kevlar. Plus, I've already administered a sedative. You should feel the effects soon enough."

"The one you gave to Kaleigh? Is that why she's unconscious?"

"I need to clear her mind before I inject her with the new elixir. It will make accommodation easier for the new occupant."

"And who won my body?" I hoped to lull him into a false sense of security and get all the answers before I smashed his face in and rendered his mouth useless.

He smirked. "No one yet. You intrigue me, Clay. I'd like to

study you further before I decide your fate, although I must admit, the fervor at the auction made the decision difficult."

"And how do you expect to...?" I broke off midsentence to yawn. Shit. So much for my plan of aggression. The sedative was starting to work. If I didn't get out of this, I could end up a prisoner in my own mind. If another deity took up residence in my body, they wouldn't be interested in restoring the Castle and enjoying a beer on the balcony. They'd want this resurrection in order to continue the destruction they didn't get a chance to finish during their last go-round on earth. My body would carry on living without me, doing things I'd never do. Hurting people I'd never hurt. And the deity would likely benefit from my extra dose of power. I'd take Camryn's serene coma any day of the week over this fresh hell.

My head nearly exploded at the thought of the coma victims.

The baku wasn't in town because of me. I'd bet good goddess-auction money that Dr. Edmonds was responsible for the creature's presence. He intended to use the baku to wipe the mind of his victim, to make room for the deity's consciousness. The creature must've escaped from the lab earlier in the week and wreaked havoc on unsuspecting residents until they recaptured it, which was the reason it didn't show up when I summoned it at the crossroads. The creature was already safely back at the compound by then, ready to devour the hopes and dreams of Magnarella's victims.

I had to keep the baku from clearing Kaleigh's mind. If Alakshmi took over, the whole town was in danger.

Struggling to remain semiconscious, I wiggled my fingers toward the lump in my pocket but to no avail. I was strapped down too tightly and too weak from the sedative to break free.

Then it occurred to me. The children didn't hold the talismans as they slept to summon the baku. They kept them on their bedside tables. As long as the talisman was appurtenant to my body, it should still work.

I focused on the talisman as my body slipped further into a relaxed state. Shadows crept through my mind, multiplying and spreading like a plague. In the dark corner, a new silhouette took shape. The creature seemed to remember our last interaction. It stopped a safe distance away and contemplated me.

"Hi, honey. I'm home," I said. *And I'm not going anywhere.*

The baku grunted. It wasn't going to back down this time. It wanted the contents of my mind, and it wanted them badly.

"How does it feel to want?" I asked.

The baku lifted its trunk and started to suck. The pressure was more intense this time, likely because I was sedated. It would be more difficult to resist.

But not impossible.

I was, after all, Melinoe reborn. Goddess of nightmares and ghosts. Bringer of madness.

I conjured a typical human nightmare—someone being buried alive. Nails raked the inside of the coffin as the person realized their oxygen was running low. The baku devoured the image whole, so I switched to another one. A drowning. Kaleigh covered by spiders. Nana Pratt in a pit of snakes. Each horrific thought was another layer for the baku to chew through to get to me. Like any creature after a massive feast, eventually the baku would be forced to rest. Its defenses would be down; maybe by then I'd have enough energy to kill it.

I had to try. Lives depended on it.

I continued to conjure the old faithfuls. A car careening off a cliff and plunging into icy waters below. Hailey Jones naked in front of library patrons. Bodily mutilation. Falling from a building.

The baku ate them piece by horrible piece.

I felt my strength waning. If I didn't act soon, I'd be god

fodder, which would've made me laugh if the consequences weren't so dire.

The baku lumbered toward the next nightmare. It seemed to be slowing down, taking longer to devour each obstacle. From the corner of my mind, I watched and waited.

Finally, the baku slowed to a halt. I sprang from a crouched position and attacked. The baku swung its trunk and smacked me to the ground. The impact rattled my teeth. As I crawled to my feet, the trunk wrapped around my body and attempted to squeeze the life out of me.

I gripped the trunk with both hands and squeezed. I wasn't sure whether there were any bones to break. If it was only cartilage, I was in trouble.

The cracking sound was music to my ears. The creature let loose a high-pitched shriek and released its hold on me. I elbowed the baku in the eye, and it fell onto its hind legs. I climbed on its back and wrestled the creature the rest of the way to the ground. I wrapped my legs around its neck and attempted to use them as a vice. I had to give the baku credit, it was tough.

But I was tougher.

I heard the crack of bone, and the baku slumped over. People often say if you die in your dreams, you'll die in real life, which isn't necessarily true.

Unless you're a baku.

I climbed off the limp body and nudged it with my foot. No reaction. Magnarella got his death match after all. Too bad he missed the show.

I couldn't leave the baku to rot in my mind or I risked irreparable damage.

It was time to wake up.

I pictured Pops standing beside me, encouraging me to persevere. He hadn't always chosen the kindest words, but I knew that had been his own history coming to the forefront.

"You cry, you die."

"Move it or lose it, Lorelei."

Never had the words rang truer.

I pictured the lab. The table I'd been strapped to. The layout of the room. I conjured a door in my mind and painted it red. I jiggled the handle. Locked.

This was the price I paid for suppressing my powers on a regular basis. I was out of practice. I had to exert more energy.

There weren't many supernaturals that could move between realms without an access point. There were even fewer that could move between realities.

Thank the gods I was one of them.

Pain seared my skull as I dragged the baku's limp carcass into reality. I clenched my teeth and fought a second wave of pain that nearly immobilized me.

I opened my eyes and recognized my surroundings. Still in the lab. Good. The baku's body rested on the white tile floor next to my table. Blood and guts seeped from the carcass. That would leave a stain on the pristine floor.

Kaleigh was still unconscious on the other table. No one was monitoring us. Bless Dr. Edmonds' giant ego.

I clenched my teeth and pulled until I broke free of the straps. Good thing I was also stronger than Kevlar.

I rushed to Kaleigh and unfastened her straps. I patted her cheeks in an effort to rouse her. No response. I'd used her fears against her in the ring. I could also use them to jolt her awake.

There are certain types of nightmares that occur during the transitional period between sleep and wakefulness. Unfortunately, these tend to be of the more intense and disturbing variety. If I could access one of Kaleigh's, though, I might be able to trigger her to wake up.

I accessed her mind, chose the most realistic and intense option, and set the nightmare loose. This was no time to be gentle. Like my actions in the ring, I took no pleasure in it.

I waited beside her, holding her hand. Her eyes flew open, and she bolted upright in a panic, breathing rapidly.

"Kaleigh, you're okay," I said in a soothing tone.

It took her a minute to come down to earth. She blinked and looked around the lab. "Where am I?" Her gaze snagged on the dead baku. "What in the hell is that thing?"

I explained the situation as quickly as I could, stressing the need for urgency.

"I'm sorry I nearly killed you," she said.

"And I'm sorry I tortured you."

She glanced at the baku's corpse. "You made up for it."

"You need to go now. I'll take care of the rest."

Kaleigh glanced at the monitor. "I might feel better if I break a few things on the way out."

"Have at it. Just don't take too long. I want you gone when the shit hits the fan." Things were about to get messy.

Kaleigh didn't hesitate. If there was a machine, she smashed it. If there was a bag of fluid, she emptied it. We'd set their little avatar project back years. I wasn't naive enough to believe it would be permanent though. Magnarella clearly had the funds, but recreating this would take time.

I lifted the baku by its tail and dragged it across the floor, leaving a trail of bodily fluids in its wake. I mentally apologized to the cleaner.

The door was unlocked. Men and their sheer arrogance never ceased to amaze me, especially after they'd already dealt with the escaped baku. I guess they figured I wasn't as smart.

Their mistake.

I carted the baku's body down the long corridor and through the wing of the compound until I reached the foyer of the main house. A butler moved to intercept me, took one look at my unwelcome package, and walked away at a brisk pace.

I heard the sound of polite laughter tinkling from the

dining room. Mr. Magnarella was entertaining company. Humiliations galore. Perfect.

Another member of staff caught me before I reached the door. Linda, the assistant I'd met the day I came for lunch. She was less fazed by the sight of my delivery than the butler —because woman.

"I'm here to see your boss."

"I'm afraid he's having brunch with guests at the moment. Do you have an appointment?"

I was impressed by her composure. "No." I shook the end of the baku's limp body. "But I think he'll want to see me regardless. I have to return an item I borrowed. It's defective."

The look on my face seemed to penetrate her thick layer of professionalism because she wisely ducked out of the way. "Do me a favor and give me a head start," she whispered. "I don't want him to know I was here."

I nodded and stood with my hand poised to turn the knob. Once she disappeared around the corner, I pushed open the double doors and strode into the room, still dragging the baku behind me. The room fell silent as I approached the table. I heaved the corpse onto the table and watched it land next to the breadbasket. A woman screamed.

I leveled Magnarella with a look that would've melted glass. "If you ever come near me, Dusty, or Kaleigh again, you'll find yourself on a platter on this very table with an apple shoved into every available orifice. Understood?"

Somebody cleared their throat.

Magnarella looked at me. Even without showing his fangs, I could feel the anger and hostility emanating from him. He wanted to kill me right here, right now.

I'd like to see you try, buddy.

His guests must've been Very Important People because he maintained his genteel demeanor.

"Message received, Miss Clay. Until we meet again." He

gestured to a member of staff. "Clean off the table, Evander. No need to subject our guests to unnecessary germs."

I turned and marched out of the room, not bothering to close the doors behind me.

"Who was that?" I heard a lady ask in a stage whisper.

"A disgruntled employee," the vampire replied. "Nothing to be concerned about. Another mimosa, Pippa?"

There was no sign of Kaleigh when I exited the compound, but the gates were open, which was a good sign. Hopefully, she'd leave town and never look back.

The sun was shining as I passed through the gates. Even in my red T-shirt and shorts, I didn't feel the cold. I was too invigorated by my show of strength. A car pulled alongside the curb and screeched to a halt.

Not just any car, a Rolls-Royce Ghost.

The passenger-side door popped open. "Get in," a voice commanded.

I got in. "I can't decide if your timing is impeccable or really shitty," I said.

Kane put the car in reverse and turned onto the road. "The event was chaotic. I searched everywhere to find you until I realized they'd whisked you away. I managed to recover your phone." He tossed it onto my lap. "I went back to the club to regroup and called Magnarella."

"I'm sure he was thrilled."

"He refused to take my call. I decided to let him refuse me in person."

I looked at him sideways. "You were going to violate your agreement with Magnarella for me?"

"Am I driving you home?" he asked without answering my question.

"Yes, please. In case you haven't noticed, I'm covered in blood and guts."

"Yours?"

"No. I killed the baku." I tugged the talisman from my

pocket and set it between us. "You saved me with this. Thank you."

He kept his gaze firmly on the road ahead. "You're a goddess," he finally said.

"Sort of."

"Sort of? You either are or you aren't."

I resisted the urge to vomit all over his luxury interior. "I am."

He briefly closed his eyes, appearing to digest all the information. "This is why you avoid touching me."

"A woman needs a reason?" I thought the joke would ease the tension, but Kane's jaw only tightened.

"Who are you?" he asked.

"Lorelei Clay."

His mouth pressed into a thin line.

"I'm Lorelei," I insisted.

He raked a hand through his hair. "I don't understand. Are you a paladin? An avatar?"

"I'm a freak of nature." I sank against the seat. "I'm Melinoe reborn. She doesn't share my consciousness or control me. She *is* me. I am her."

He looked struck by lightning. "A natural-born goddess."

"That's me. An incarnation." An uncontrolled birth that happens spontaneously in nature—to human parents. "Rare, but it happens."

He seemed unable to form words as he parked outside the Castle gate. I'd never seen him so disquieted. "Goddess of the dead and nightmares. This is why you can communicate with spirits."

"Among other things." My heart pounded. "Listen, Kane. I know you don't owe me anything, but I am asking you to keep this to yourself. Not even Josie can know."

"Why?"

"Do you really not understand? If word gets out, I'll have a target on my back and a hefty price on my head."

His brow furrowed. "If you're Melinoe, why can't you...?" He stopped abruptly. "You can."

"I choose to dull my shine. I didn't ask for these powers, and I try not to use them." I reached for him, intending to reassure him, but he recoiled.

"No, don't. You can't."

Confusion threaded through my thoughts. "I don't understand."

"And I can't explain it to you. Now you know how it feels." He reached across me and opened the door, leaving the scent of musk, sandalwood, and pine in his wake. "Good-bye, Miss... Melinoe."

"My name is Lorelei," I insisted, as I exited the car.

Without another word, he pulled the door shut and drove away.

CHAPTER 20

A figure in a black coat awaited me on the front porch. Naomi Smith.

And the hits keep on coming.

"Long night?" she asked, as I trudged up the steps to the porch.

"I thought we were finished," I said.

"So did I, until I saw you at the event."

Worst fear confirmed. "I drank an elixir just like the other contestant."

She stared at me for a long, uncomfortable moment. "My real name is Eunomia," she finally said.

"I can see why you stick with Naomi."

"That name doesn't mean anything to you?"

"Should it?"

"Eunomia is the goddess of law and order."

"How about that? It's like your parents knew you'd want to grow up to be an investigator."

"I chose my own name for this vessel." She paused. "I think you're like me."

"I don't think so. I'm not very into law and order."

She gave me a pointed look. "You know what I mean. I have to tell you; The Corporation is going to be very interested in you."

I could practically hear Matilda's voice in my head, urging me to slay this woman where she stands. Naomi, or Eunomia, threatened my peaceful existence. The goddess seemed to read my mind.

"If you're thinking about killing me, I'd advise against it. I have a report with your name ready to send up the chain of command should anything happen to me. If I go missing, they'll come directly to your door."

"For the record, I didn't kill Bruce. Your employers were responsible for that."

"Mr. Huang knew the risks of his post."

I felt stuck. I'd hurt enough living creatures in the past twenty-four hours. "I'm not what you think," I said. "Just file your original report and forget the rest."

Naomi ignored my request. "What's the point of living this quiet life in the middle of nowhere when you're a goddess? Use your powers like the rest of us as part of The Corporation."

"My powers were temporary. They came from the elixir."

"That's not what I heard."

"You heard wrong."

"Who administered your soma?" Naomi pressed. "I don't know how you've managed to escape our notice all these years. I thought we had better scouts."

Because my grandfather worked very hard to protect me. He knew the kind of life that awaited me if my identity were discovered. He didn't want that for me, and neither did I.

I said none of that to Naomi, though. I wasn't willing to give up my secret to an organization like The Corporation.

"I don't even know what soma is." Okay, that was a lie. Soma was a ritual drink that was said to offer immortality and other godly powers. It was basically the same concept as Dr. Edmonds's second elixir.

"The Corporation offers a life of luxury and security," Naomi continued. "You'd be able to climb out of this money pit of despair."

That hurt. "Hey, it's a work in progress."

She inclined her head toward the Castle. "Good thing you're set to live a long life because you'll spend most of it on this renovation project."

There was one question I had for Naomi. "Is The Corporation involved with Dr. Edmonds?"

"He is no longer in our employ. From what I understand, he was unhappy with his clearance level and left to pursue his interests elsewhere about a year ago."

In other words, he knew The Corporation was creating avatars but didn't know how and decided to branch out on his own when they wouldn't tell him. Enter Magnarella.

"Let them know he'll be pursuing those interests from scratch," I said, unlocking the front door. "His lab may have experienced some technical difficulties."

Naomi's mouth quirked. "My employers will be happy to hear it."

I looked at her. "I'm not like you, Naomi. What you saw during that fight was the elixir, and now that it's left my body, I'm back to being me. Believe me or don't, but please leave me out of any report to The Corporation. I just want to live a life in peace."

Naomi considered me. "Very well. If you ever change your mind, give us a call. Good luck to you, Miss Clay."

Weary and weak, I retreated inside my Castle. Relief washed over me at the sight of Renee descending the staircase in a stupor. Dr. Edmonds had chosen the baku, likely because he believed the creature was incapable of being killed and there was no danger of his victims' minds being restored. It seemed I'd identified the flaw in his plan.

"You're awake," I said.

Renee gazed at me. "What on earth happened?"

"Long story."

Alicia ran down the stairs behind her mother, still clad in the rumpled clothes she'd slept in. "Mom's awake!"

I smiled. "I can see that."

"What'd you do?" Alicia asked me.

Renee's brow furrowed. "Honey, Lorelei isn't a doctor."

Alicia threw her arms around her mother's waist and squeezed. "I'm so glad you're awake."

Renee kissed the top of her daughter's head. "Me, too."

I turned on my phone to see a series of messages from Gunther. Dusty was no longer a swan and Camryn was awake.

Hallelujah.

After a scalding shower, I was torn between sleep and food. Maybe I'd drag a chicken drumstick to my sleeping bag and call it a day.

I slept for the next ten hours. When I finally awoke, Renee and Alicia were gone. They'd left behind cartons of Chinese food for me. Very considerate.

My thoughts turned to Kane. I hated that the demon was angry with me. I never wanted that.

I picked up my phone and called the Devil's Playground. Josie picked up on the second ring.

"Josie, it's Lorelei. Can I please speak to Kane?"

"He isn't here."

"Do you know where he is?"

"Not here."

I sighed. "Do you know when he'll be back?"

"He didn't say."

"It's important that I speak with him. If you know where he is…"

"If I know and I'm not telling you, it's because he asked me not to. You should know by now where my loyalty lies."

"Do you know why he left?"

Josie's silence answered that question.

"Fine. Will you tell him I called, and that I'd really like to see him?"

"I wouldn't hold your breath," the vampire said.

"Bite me." I hung up the phone, fighting a surge of emotions. It wasn't as though I lied to him about my identity. He knew I was hiding a secret, and now that he knew what that secret was, how could he not understand why I had to keep it from him? My identity posed a threat to everyone around me. I came to Fairhaven to live a quiet life where nobody cared that I was a goddess reborn. Where I was simply Lorelei Clay, an introvert with a fondness for renovation projects and cheap beer.

My mistake had been getting too close to other residents. I shouldn't have helped Steven and Ashley. I should've ordered Nana Pratt and Ray to cross over along with the other spirits. They'd grown comfortable at the Castle and even worse, they'd grown attached to me. Alicia too. Her mother was right to tell me off. I had no business inserting myself in that girl's life.

The ward activated, and I dragged myself to the window. There was no one there. Odd.

I opened the door to see a note stuck to it.

You've made a dangerous enemy.

"At least it isn't a horse's head." I crumpled the note in my hand.

"Is that from the mobster?" Ray asked, appearing on the porch.

"He didn't sign it, but all signs point to yes." I carried the wad of paper to the kitchen and tossed it in the trashcan.

"You're not worried?" Ray asked. "I'd be shaking in my boots after a warning like that."

"I'll be fine, Ray. I've got on my big girl pants and everything. No need to worry about me."

"You might want to invest in an extra one of those magic wards, just to be on the safe side."

"You're right."

Ray gave me a fatherly smile. "I'm always right, Lorelei. When will you accept my nuggets of wisdom?"

"How about I start tomorrow? I'm still beat."

"Sleep well," Ray said. "You've earned it."

"Is that your way of thanking me for helping Renee?"

He wrapped his arms around me, and I felt the light pressure of his ghostly arms. "Thank you," he whispered.

I climbed the staircase, acutely aware of the sound of my heart raging in my chest. I counted each step as I made my way to my bedroom in an effort to stay grounded and not give in to the discomfort slowly building inside me. Ray was right about the ward—I'd have to find the money for a stronger one, or barter with Phaedra Bridger. An alert was no longer sufficient.

I stripped off my clothes and tossed them into the laundry basket. Like the victims of the baku, I was still bone tired after ten hours of sleep, which didn't happen very often. The death match and its aftermath were finally catching up with me. Ray was right about that, too.

I turned on the hot water in the shower and let the steam penetrate my skin. I couldn't wait to scrub myself clean of the last week. Try as I might to act calm and collected, I knew in my gut Ray was wrong about one thing—Magnarella's note wasn't a warning.

It was a promise.

———

Lorelei's story continues in **Dead Wrong**, book 4 in the *Crossroads Queen* series.

• • •

To join my VIP list and download an extended scene from Kane's POV in Chapter 6 of *Dead to the World,* visit https://annabelchase.com/dead-to-the-world-offer.

ALSO BY ANNABEL CHASE

While you're waiting for the next book, please sure to sign up for my newsletter at www.annabelchase.com and check out my other series:

Midnight Empire series

Pandora's Pride

Federal Bureau of Magic

Starry Hollow Witches

Magic Bullet

Spellbound/Spellbound Ever After

Spellslingers Academy

Demonspawn Academy

The Bloomin' Psychic

Divine Place

Midlife Magic Cocktail Club

Hex Support

Made in United States
Troutdale, OR
01/18/2025

28062267R00141